An Eternal Affair

Scriptures and Encouragement to Carry You
throughout Your Journey with Jesus

HELENE MARIE CRUZ

WestBow
PRESS
A DIVISION OF THOMAS NELSON

Scripture quotations taken from the Amplified® Bible, Copyright © 1954, 1958, 1962, 1964, 1965, 1987 by The Lockman Foundation Used by permission. (www.Lockman.org)

Scripture quotations taken from the King James Version, KJV Large Print Compact Bible Copyright © 2000 by Holman Bible Publishers All rights reserved

Scriptures quotations taken from THE HOLY BIBLE, NEW INTERNATIONAL VERSION®, NIV® Copyright © 1973, 1978, 1984, 2011 by Biblica, Inc.™ Used by permission. All rights reserved worldwide

WestBow Press books may be ordered through booksellers or by contacting:

WestBow Press
A Division of Thomas Nelson
1663 Liberty Drive
Bloomington, IN 47403
www.westbowpress.com
1-(866) 928-1240

ISBN: 978-1-4497-6873-7 (hc)
ISBN: 978-1-4497-6872-0 (sc)
ISBN: 978-1-4497-6876-8 (e)

Library of Congress Control Number: 2012917589

Printed in the United States of America

WestBow Press rev. date: 11/01/2012

Contents

Dedication

This book is dedicated to my beloved and selfless mother, Linda Jean Goldstein Cruz (January 3, 1948–December 23, 2009). "Mama Cruz" would laugh when I would do an essay for school and count my words to make sure I had the exact amount required—nothing more, nothing less. Now, I am writing a book and can't stop writing! Thank you for sacrificing everything for all of us. I miss you daily, but it brings me peace knowing that you are having an "eternal affair"!

I also dedicate this book to Elvera Lucy Di Conza Goldstein, aka "Granny" (June 16, 1916–October 18, 2011). We went through a lot together; you drove us crazy, but we loved you so much. This book was written during the summer that you became ill. I didn't know the Lord was preparing me to lose someone so special but start on an amazing journey in the process. Life on earth will *never* be the same without you.

Acknowledgments

Of course, I would like to thank the "Tremendous Trio"—God, Jesus, and Holy Spirit (Father, Son, and Counselor), without whom this book would not have been possible.

I would like to thank my family, my heart—a true blessing--Papa Cruz, Mark, Lisa, Tony and Gianna (aka Punki); Rick, Steve, Beverly and Vicky Huber--a special extension of our immediate family; The Sangiorgios, my spiritual family, whose door is always open to me; my prayer partners who intercede for me on a regular basis and have endlessly lifted this book up to the Lord with me (Susan Graham-John, Rev. Nancy Martinez, Dr. Sandra Bond, Minister Derrick Jones, Mama Edith Wilson, Sisters Sonia Arenas, Elizabeth Birru-Burnett, Sabrina Hines and Sofia Varela). A special thanks to Chelsea Ruffino who photographed me with her sweet spirit and great talent. And for all of the family in Christ who aid me in my journey daily and have stood by me from the beginning, especially in the darkest hours of my life—you know who you are and I thank you from the bottom of my heart. May God bless each and every person mentioned and all those who are in my heart, keeping you covered under His mighty wings.

Introduction

I was raised in a working class neighborhood by both of my parents in a loving and fun home. My father is from Puerto Rico (a mix of African, Spaniard and Taino Indian) and my mother was European-American; her maternal grandparents hailed from Italy and her paternal grandparents were Jews who migrated from Russia and Poland. I remember my parents' experiencing conflict in the early years of their marriage, in an age when interracial marriages were not common (1960s and 1970s). I believe that being multicultural *and* biracial affected my self-esteem in that I never felt that I really belonged to any one group. My father is a dark-skinned Latino (*un trigueño*), and my mother was a fair-skinned Caucasian. They married in 1967, when this union was not as acceptable as it is now, in 2011. Therefore, when I was growing up, I did not feel accepted by people whose families were culturally and racially homogeneous. I also went to elementary school with classmates who were mostly Irish-American and Italian-American, but I came from a neighborhood that had many African-Americans and Latinos living in it, so there was a culture clash there, too, for me growing up in the 1970s and 1980s.

In addition, I became the proverbial "middle child" that we read about, longing for attention (growing up with my older sister, younger brother, and two older cousins who spent a lot of time with us). My nickname was Tiger in the early years of my life, and I probably don't have to explain why. I always tried to be loved, got in the middle of the games, and wanted to be "invited to the party" all the time, sometimes being a little dramatic and hard to manage. When I wasn't included or accepted, I felt unloved and lacked worth. I believe those feelings carried with me throughout the years. However, these many years later, I know with confidence that my worth does not depend on others but only one—Jesus!

I attended a Catholic elementary school and high school and was a good student, keeping up those good grades in college and graduate school. I attended church on a regular basis with my grandmother and sister for many years. Even though, on the surface, I appeared happy and was a "good kid," I always felt that there was something missing. Growing up, I knew people who were Christians and thought that they were brainwashed; I already knew (or thought I knew) the Lord because I grew up as a Catholic and had the foundation of Christianity. I did not understand this "salvation" thing, and Christians seemed so fanatical to me. My understanding was that if you were good, you would go to heaven, regardless of your religion. I thought that these Christians were down and out, reaching for a crutch out of desperation, but today I know that Jesus is the only way to eternal life. It was their zeal and joy that I was seeing but could not identify with, but now I have experienced it for myself.

In the meantime, prior to my conversion almost thirteen years ago, I was one who liked to organize and attend parties in my twenties (and early thirties, too); I was the friend who could not wait for the next party. I loved to have many people around me. My motto back then could have been "quantity is better than quality." It is the reverse for me now—I prefer the quality and depth of my relationship with Jesus and the intimacy with family and close friends as opposed to the noise, busyness, and emptiness of the party scene and having to have so many people around me in a superficial way. In my twenties, having a good time was a priority, and that involved dancing, drinking, and meeting guys who weren't really looking for a commitment, just a good time. In the midst of such an empty lifestyle, God always kept me covered under His protective wing. I was associated with people who did drugs and got drunk on a regular basis, but the Lord always kept me from experimenting too much. I guess I had that fear of God in me, but I also did not ever want to lose control and wind up addicted. I did not do drugs, nor did I drink to the point of intoxication.

I constantly thank God that He pulled me out of situations that were not good for me during this time in my life, even though I had many fun times along the way. I met people then who are still in my life now. However, God had better things in store for me; I just couldn't see it then. He always made sure that no one hurt me and that I never got drunk, high, abused, or raped by the guys I would meet who just wanted to use me. God always put me first, all the time. Unfortunately, back then, I called upon Him only when I needed something—I used God, which is what many people do. Now I call upon Him first, just to thank Him and just to praise Him. In fact, God is the first person I call upon in the morning, during the day, in the evening—even if it is just to say "I love you" and "Thank you."

Around the time that I started my graduate school program in 1994, I met a handful of Christians both in the workplace and at school who were different from the ones previously mentioned. They never preached condemnation to me and didn't judge me. In fact, they answered questions when I had them and showed me love, unlike some of the Christians I had met earlier in life, who were very condemning and arrogant. In fact, these people are still in my life, over seventeen years later, and are now part of my spiritual family.

On October 25, 1998, I was visiting a coworker at her house in St. James, New York, for the weekend. She had grown up in a Christian home, and her parents shared their testimonies with me that morning at the breakfast table. They asked me if I wanted to have the Lord in my heart, and I responded, "Yes." So, I became saved—a born-again Christian. But I did not know what that truly meant. Nevertheless, that was the turning point in my life, the one that changed my eternal destiny. I didn't know what was in store for me!

Soon, I became fearful that I would be like the Christians I had met earlier in my life—very preachy, condemning, and arrogant—and did not want to give up total control of my life to God. I thought that I could never enjoy secular (non-Christian) things again because I was "in the Lord." I did not understand that God deals with everyone differently and that all Christians are not alike. He has plans for each one of us (Jer. 29:11), and there are things that He wants each of us to abandon, as well as other things that He wants us to take up. But God has to speak to each of us individually when He knows we can receive what He is instructing.

Right after I asked God into my heart that October morning, He started to get my attention, dealing with me on various issues such as arrogance, jealousy, lust, malice, lack of commitment, selfishness, superficiality, materialism, greed, and debt. For the next four years or so, I still did the party thing, but my spirit was different. I started feeling convicted about doing things that were not in alignment with God's Word, and those very same things no longer gave me pleasure. Certain people and activities in my life had to go, and I gave them up with a sense of peace. There was no room for people who and things that did not fit my new walk because, where there is a godly spirit, ungodliness has to leave.

In 2001, right before 9/11, I experienced this burden that something big was going to happen and that my life would change. Tragedy struck our nation, and one of my friend's brothers was killed in the Twin Towers. I believe that was when I really handed my life over to God. I realized that we can be taken in a matter of seconds, that God is in total control, and that my life and my heart had to be surrendered completely to God. I started ministering to my circle of friends who experienced grief from this loss, and it was then that I realized that I needed to be around more Christians. I rededicated my life to God the day of the 9/11 memorial service, November 17, 2001, when the altar call was given, and I have not been the same since. A few months later, the Lord opened up a door for me to work at Pace University, my undergraduate alma mater, in their Career Services Office, which was a blessing (and a ministry) in and of itself. Throughout my years there, the Lord has allowed me to pray, encourage, lay healing hands, evangelize, and even witness to some in the Pace community.

I needed a home church in 2001 after I rededicated myself to my walk with Christ. I prayed for one, and then, a year later, a friend introduced me to Christ Tabernacle. I started attending in September 2002, and it was a training ground for me in terms of growing in the Lord, fellowshipping with other Christians in our church family, and also serving the Lord. One year after I started attending, I became baptized via water immersion (as opposed to the christening that I was given as an infant in the Roman Catholic Church), and I then began serving as a presenter of career development workshops within the church's youth ministry, which is known as Youth Explosion. A few years later, I became involved with our church's Organizational Development Team, which provided coaching on leadership and staff development. I was called upon to head up a series of workshops called the Four Levels of Leadership under our church's Leadership Academy, which allowed the facilitators and me to bring secular concepts and theories from corporate training programs to the church but present our materials from a godly perspective, providing appropriate Scriptures and references to biblical leaders—the most important leader being Jesus, who was a *servant* leader.

I could go on and on about the rest of my testimony and what the Lord has done, but I will save that for later in the book. In these past thirteen years, I have learned that God is in control. I have to surrender to Him every day and wait on His will and timing. He has blessed me with every relationship, every job, every friend, everything I am, and everything I have. And for that I am truly grateful. I continue to wait on His timing, but in this process I have learned that I would rather have God's perfect will than God's permissive will for my life in every aspect. God's perfect will is *much better* than Helene's will. God will "permit" us to have our own way if we twist His arm hard enough!

I have also learned that there can be no other gods beside or before Him. For example, growing up as a Catholic, I would pray to my favorite saints for protection against harm, depression, sickness, and so on. Also, I would depend on material things—sometimes people, activities, and relationships—to keep me at peace. But as the years have passed and my fellowship with the Lord has become stronger each day, I have discovered that God, through his Son Jesus and the Holy Spirit as my "internal counselor," are a three-in-one package; there is no need for any other gods, idols, or practices. No one can give you the peace, joy, and righteousness that the Lord gives each day.

God is present even when the storms of life are blowing. He has definitely changed my heart. I find myself to be more giving of my time, my money, my attention, and my prayers for others, as well as more tolerant of and patient with others than I have ever been in all of my life. When I find myself going back to old patterns of complaining, criticizing, gossiping, or getting in worry mode, I quickly feel the Holy Spirit pulling on the inside of me, telling me that does not fit who God wants me to be, and I start to pray for change.

Granted, there are still areas of my life that need sanctification (to be made holy, to be cleansed). I will explain this more fully later in the "Trust, Obey and Forgive" chapter of the book. The Lord still deals with me on fully surrendering to Him, trusting Him completely, and also being obedient in my walk, for the flesh can be very weak. Forgiveness is another issue that keeps resurfacing. Just when you think that you have made peace with something or someone, unforgiveness rears its ugly head. I am constantly asking the Lord to guard my heart against those thoughts and feelings.

This book is a result of a seed that was planted in my early Pace days. I was talking with my father about a guest speaker who was coming to promote his new career-related book to our MBA students. Papa Cruz (the name I use to refer to him when speaking to others) turned to me and said, "Hey, why don't you write a book?" That concept was so foreign to me because I had only been working in the industry for a couple of years and did not think I had enough expertise to pull it off. A year or so later, my colleague, who is a believer (follower of Jesus Christ), came into the office and told me that she had had a dream about me. She said that, in the dream, I was making copies of my work. I had written lots of articles and was moving on to do some consulting. Specifically, she said that I was moving on to something "really big." Again, I dismissed it, not thinking that I was at the level necessary to be published. A few years later, I was asked to speak at a conference sponsored by a national, nonprofit organization based in Washington, DC. The conference coordinator and I were discussing compensation for the event, and she said that because a nonprofit organization was sponsoring the conference, there was no budget to pay the presenters. However, she did mention that she had read a few of my articles that had been published in the *Wall Street Journal* and suggested that I bring any books I had authored to the conference to sell them after each conference session, which would be a platform for me to earn money. Again, the book theme had come up, and I came up empty. I did not have any books to sell—yet!

Then a word was prophesied over me, and that birthed this project. Some of my female colleagues and I were invited to attend Peekskill Christian Center's Women's Fellowship on a cold Saturday morning, February 12, 2011. Although it was early in the morning, the three of us were pumped to hear Dr. Bond lead a Bible study and perhaps prophesy, as she has done at her church and also at previous ministerial events. Sure enough, we received a great word from the Lord through her. Dr. Bond also felt led by the Holy Spirit to prophesy to certain people in the room. As we were getting closer to the end of the fellowship, she just kept feeling led to continue to speak to the women there, for which God gave words of encouragement and direction using Dr. Bond as a vessel. Dr. Bond approached me and asked, "Do you write?" Being literal sometimes, I answered no because I haven't written with my hands in years, but I do a heck of a lot of word processing on the computer. She looked at me and continued to share that the Lord was showing her a book for me to write and that the Lord would give me its title in three days. She also said, "Thus saith the Lord," which, to me, is the Lord speaking and confirming that this is definitely *from Him,* not her will or mine. Well, I looked at her and my colleagues, my sisters in the faith, and was a bit overwhelmed. Dr. Bond gave me a few other messages that I will share later, but concerning the book, she confirmed that I have a lot to share and that I would be doing so in the book, which will be a blessing others.

Three days later, I was up early in the morning, which is when I usually do my praise, worship, and prayer time before the workday starts. It was a cloudy day, and I looked out my window. As the worship music played, I looked up to heaven and thought, *Lord, what goes on up there?* I thought of my beloved mother, who had died a little over a year earlier, and I was missing her very much. I thanked God for that wonderful mother and for the privilege of leading her to Christ before she died so that I could know she was up there rejoicing. I just wanted to know what she was doing up there with the Lord and the others who had gone before her. I thought, *What a love affair God wants to have with us!* We will definitely have that direct physical contact with the Lord when we are in heaven, which is really an "eternal affair," starting from when we receive Christ and lasting *forever.* In that moment, *An Eternal Affair* was put on my spirit as the title of the book about which Dr. Bond had prophesied.

For me, the word *affair* had a negative connotation because it is often used in terms of people having affairs, namely, extramarital ones. I had to wrap my mind around this word in order to move forward with the title. A love affair is not a bad thing as long as it is in alignment with the will of God. And a love affair with the Lord is the ultimate, infinite affair. I proceeded to check the Internet to see if anyone else had written a book with the same name, and there was nothing like it out there (although there is a recorded CD by artist Heather B with the title *Eternal Affairs*). I claimed the title in my mind and heart and started praying about writing the book.

So, here I am, seven months later, responding to the prompting of the Holy Spirit and writing what the Lord wants me to share in order to not only encourage and evangelize but also to help others (and myself) be restored, knowing that this walk on earth goes by really quickly. It is only a snap of one's finger in comparison to eternity, and I want every reader of this book to share eternity with the Lord.

Throughout this book, I will present Scriptures that have been critical in my life, life-changing Scriptures that have carried me through the storms of life. I will share some of my life experiences as they are related to things that I learned in ministry or through family experiences, work, relationships, school, teaching, and so on. You won't get too much of my life story—I will save that for the books to come (in the name of Jesus).

Everything that we need to know in life is in God's instruction manual—the Bible—so I strongly recommend that you read the Word of God daily. Each Scripture is taken from one of the following versions of the Bible: King James Version (KJV), the Amplified Bible (AMP), and the New International Version (NIV). These Scriptures (as well as the rest of the Word of God) will carry you throughout your journey with Jesus on this earth once you become born again. I will be explaining that concept in Chapter 1. Once we have that conversion experience, then we journey in our "affair" with Him through life, from here to eternity (like the title of the movie from the 1950s). And now, let's begin what I call *An Eternal Affair*.

CHAPTER 1

For God So Loved the World ...

"For God so greatly loved and dearly prized the world that He [even] gave up His only begotten (unique) Son, so that whoever believes in (trusts in, clings to, relies on) Him shall not perish (come to destruction, be lost) but have eternal (everlasting) life" (John 3:16 AMP). Before we get into any other Scriptures in the Bible, we must start with the most important one, which speaks of the salvation of man through the coming of the Lord, Jesus Christ (the Son of God), in order to walk among man, go to the cross, die for our sins and bury them, and then be resurrected to be seated at God's right hand forever.

The Gospel of John is one of most precious books in the Bible because John writes about his intimate walk with the Savior, but more important, he explains to us what it means to be "born again," to enter a state of spiritual being that affects us eternally. For many walking this earth, it is merely a concept or a theory—something that seems like a religious exercise or an option for some to get to heaven. Some even consider "born again" to be a separate Christian denomination. The third chapter of John explains this concept, which is really so much more than that—it is our gift of salvation, a free gift, one that changes our eternal destiny. As Jesus explained to Nicodemus, one cannot be born again in a literal sense because we cannot shrink back to six- or seven-pound babies (or, these days, nine- or ten-pound babies) and go back into our mothers' wombs. It is a spiritual state of being, a process by which we realize that Jesus Christ came to this earth for the purpose of showing us the Father, carrying our sins—all of our sins, every sin, the sin of mankind—and nailing every sin to the cross as He was crucified. He came to die so that He could be resurrected and we could therefore live forever with Him and the Father in paradise. It is a conversion process in which we admit that we have sinned and have fallen short of the glory of God (Rom. 3:23 NIV), even though we are being "the best that we can be." We have to come to terms with the notion that being the best or even being good is really very subjective and does not apply in God's economy in terms of getting you into heaven. God's gift to us is objective—open to anyone on this planet who wants to receive it, without measure of one person being "better than" another or one person's good works outweighing his or her brother's works. We cannot buy our tickets into heaven by being good or performing good works. It is by our faith in Christ as our Savior and our complete surrender to Him that we make it to heaven and our names are written in the Lamb's Book of Life (Rev. 3:20 NIV).

We are born again, or rebirthed, as some Christian denominations call it (or "saved," as we term it because we have received salvation) when we go to the cross. I don't mean that we literally go to the cross because Jesus was nailed to the cross *for* us. It means that we just simply put everything out there to the Lord, surrendering our wills and our lives, and we ask God to forgive us for the past and present sins that we have committed, as well as the future sins that we will commit and cannot yet even imagine. Since Jesus was already sent to pay the debt for *all* man in full, we do not need to live with the shame and guilt of our sins—He already died to erase the shame and guilt from our lives. How amazing is that?

Prior to my salvation and even in the first few years of my walk with the Lord, I was very uncomfortable with the phrase "born again" because of the Christians I had known. They were very preachy, fanatical, arrogant Christians who sounded more like the Pharisees and the Sadducees (the Jewish leaders) of Jesus' day than the Lord Himself. I really had to get over that and claim who I was, especially because I was now one of God's children and if I wanted to reap the benefits of being His, I had to be proud to say that I was a born-again Christian.

"I am the way, the truth and the life. No one comes to the Father except through me" (John 14:6 NIV). Many believe that there are several ways to get to heaven because many religions exist in the world that claim to take us there by works. Christianity is the only religion that takes us to heaven by faith—it is not by what we can do but by what Jesus has already done! It is not God's will for us to believe in whatever sounds or feels right or whatever promises us peace and joy at the moment. Our beliefs have to be in alignment with His Word—the Old and the New Testaments, which were written by godly men and women under the direction of the Holy Spirit. [We will talk about the third part of the Godhead, the Holy Spirit, throughout the rest of the book, but know that with God, you get a three-in-one deal—Father (God), Son (Jesus), and Counselor (Holy Spirit).]

God created the world and loves everyone in it, even those who we consider unworthy or "disqualified" because they are not good in man's eyes. God's love is so strong (actually, God *is* love!) that He decided to send His Son to earth to live as a human, to live a humble life (when He didn't have to, for He was a king on the throne in the heavens). Despite Jesus' humble beginnings—being born in a manger (stable) to parents who had to flee their homeland—He had an amazing ministry in the last years of His earthly life. Jesus started His ministry at age thirty and it lasted only three years, but what He accomplished in those three years was awesome—saving souls, transforming lives, laying hands on the sick for healing, performing miracles, raising people from the dead, and more. God sent Jesus because He wanted the world to know who He was *through* Jesus and to accept the prophetic word that was given to the Israelites in the following Scripture (Isa. 53 KJV):

> Who hath believed our report? And to whom is the arm of the LORD revealed? For he shall grow up before him as a tender plant, and as a root out of a dry ground: he hath no form nor comeliness; and when we shall see him, there is no beauty that we should desire him. He is despised and rejected of men; a man of sorrows, and acquainted with grief: and we hid as it were our faces from him; he was despised, and we esteemed him not. Surely he hath borne our griefs, and carried our sorrows: yet we did esteem him stricken, smitten of God, and afflicted. But he was wounded for our transgressions; he was bruised for our iniquities: the chastisement of our peace was upon him; and with his stripes we are healed. All we like sheep have gone astray; we have turned everyone to his own way; and the Lord hath laid

on him the iniquity of us all. He was oppressed, and he was afflicted, yet he opened not his mouth: he is brought as a lamb to the slaughter, and as a sheep before her shearers is dumb, so he openeth not his mouth. He was taken from prison and from judgment: and who shall declare his generation? For he was cut off out of the land of the living: for the transgression of my people was he stricken. And he made his grave with the wicked and with the rich in his death; because he had done no violence, neither was any deceit in his mouth. Yet it pleased the LORD to bruise him; he hath put him to grief: when thou shalt make his soul an offering for sin, he shall see his seed, he shall prolong his days, and the pleasure of the Lord shall prosper in his hand. He shall see of the travail of his soul, and shall be satisfied: by his knowledge shall my righteous servant justify many; for he shall bear their iniquities. Therefore will I divide him a portion with the great, and he shall divide the spoil with the strong; because he hath poured out his soul unto death: and he was numbered with the transgressors; and he bares the sin of many, and made intercession for the transgressors.

Although the Old Testament is the Word that is followed by both of the Judeo-Christian traditions, it was God's intention that *everyone* He had created would follow Him (the Lord, Jehovah) and accept His son, Jesus Christ (Emmanuel, the Anointed One) as the promised Messiah, regardless of the region of the world in which they live where there are so many other man-made religions practiced. Jesus came to save; He also came to die for all mankind (and womankind, too) so that we all can live with Him and the Father forever.

Way before God ordered the sacrificial death of Jesus or gave Isaiah the prophetic message of the Messiah, the crucifixion, and the resurrection, the Lord stated in Exodus when Moses delivered the Ten Commandments, "I am the Lord your God, who has brought you out of the land of Egypt, out of the house of bondage. You shall have no other gods before or besides Me" (Ex. 20:2–3 AMP). God is a jealous God, but not in the way that we define *jealous* because God cannot and does not sin. God simply does not want us to have any other gods before or beside Him because His spirit becomes grieved when we are deceived by other gods and when

His human creations refuse to believe, accept, follow, and serve Him and Him alone. The Amplified Bible specifically states that we (meaning all people, not just those who are saved and not just the Israelites of the Old Testament) should not have any other gods before or beside God. This means that anything that we put before or on the same level as the Lord—idols or anything that takes priority over or has more importance (or even equal importance) to God—needs to be eliminated, or it may be eliminated for us by the Lord. Please know that anything or anyone that vies for our attention with God will not be able to stand for too long—any possession, any human, any job, and so on. We are going to talk more about this in Chapter 2; there are practices that many of us, even as Christians, have been taught by our denominations over the years that we may need to address, ideologies that we need to surrender because we are placing too much attention on them, putting them before the Lord, or ranking them up there right alongside of Him.

I "dabbled" in other practices and beliefs before I came to the Lord, and even after salvation, as God was sanctifying me ("cleaning," making me holy), there were people and activities that ranked up there on the same level with the Lord in my mind, and those things had to be put in check. Granted, this did not happen overnight. God deals with us according to how we can handle His correction (called conviction). He has dealt with me on some occasions slowly, and, if I can handle it (or if I need it quickly), He addresses me on the spot, without delay.

In essence, what I am declaring is the importance of who Jesus is and who He longs to be in our lives. The beautiful difference between Christianity and all other belief systems that exist in this world is that Christianity is objective, while the others tend to be subjective. Most other practices require that their believers engage in certain practices, sometimes very ritualistic traditions that have been passed down through a number of generations, in order to gain the approval or acceptance of their god(s) or whomever or whatever they serve or worship. The emphasis is on "good works"; the question for them, which always exists and can bring some discomfort or a lack of peace, is "What must one do in order to be good in the eyes of one's supreme being?" From my observations, the main order of business for believers of other religions is the measurement of one's goodness. For starters, how does one define *good?* How good does one have to be in order to make it to heaven? Who is the measurer of that goodness, and how it is measured?

Christianity is based on faith, *not* works or what one perceives as being good. It is objective in that we simply (but wholeheartedly) profess with our mouths and believe with our hearts that Jesus is Lord, the Son of God, and that he took our place on that cross, burying our sins, so that we are forgiven for past, present, and future sins. As John 10:28 (AMP) says, "And I give them eternal life, and they shall never lose it or perish throughout the ages. [To all eternity they shall never by any means be destroyed.] And no one is able to snatch them out of My hand." Either you believe in Jesus as the Son of God, or you don't. It's just that simple; it's black and white, with no gray area. You believe either that He is the Savior or that He was a crazy man who was totally delusional, thinking that He was the Son of God. There is no in between. And there is no trying to measure how good we are. We can *never* achieve the goodness of Jesus, but through His righteousness, we are made right and accepted into God's kingdom forever! That's some incredible news, isn't it?

Jesus brings life—eternal life—and, as He said to the woman at the well, "Whoever takes a drink of the water that I will give him shall never, no never, be thirsty any more. But the water that I will give him shall become a spring of water welling up (flowing, bubbling) [continually] within him unto (into, for) eternal life" (John 4:14 AMP). Jesus didn't mean this literally but spiritually. Once you know Him and make Him the Lord of your life, you will no longer have that longing in your soul. Jesus will fill that thirst, hunger, emptiness. Only He can do this. Drugs, alcohol, other vices, relationships, success, promotions, material things, and even religion, which is defined as any ritual or tradition that is man-made, cannot fill that void. Only Jesus can complete you.

Remember the *Christ* in *Christ*ianity and know that it is Jesus we trust, upon whom we call. He is the reason for our faith and the reason that we have eternal life. Our lives on earth are but a breath; eternal life, as God truly meant for it to be for us, will be in heaven. Who doesn't want to live forever with the God who created us and the Son who sacrificed *everything* for us? So, why would we need to seek anything else, worship any other god(s), or participate in any other practices outside of those that the Lord has sanctioned in the Bible?

In terms of Jesus' sacrifice at the cross, we do not have to work off our sins or offer up any more sacrifices, as the Israelites offered the Lord in the tabernacles described in the Old Testament. We certainly do not and should not mirror (replicate) the sacrifices that the Egyptians and other groups in the Old Testament offered to their gods (little *g*), which was not pleasing to God (big *G*). And we do not have to atone for our sins because Jesus already paid the price; however, we do need to repent when we commit sin in order to restore the fellowship that we have with Him.

I once shared the following with some family members in discussing the different denominations within the Christian faith. I cannot even count how many different Christian churches there are that worship under different traditions, some even taking the Bible and adding other doctrine to it, which is very dangerous. I explained that when God greets you in heaven, He is not going to ask you for your ID card showing what denomination you belonged to or ask if you were a Catholic, a Pentecostal, a Baptist, or an Evangelical. All that matters is that you truly received Jesus, His Son, the Savior of the world, into your heart and that your life was a reflection of that relationship. There is no holding cell or waiting room between heaven and hell where you will have to be purged of or work off your sins before being admitted to heaven. Again, Jesus paid that price for you on Calvary at the cross; therefore, you will never be "good enough" to save yourself. All you have to do is receive Christ's gift of salvation—while you are on this earth, of course; you can't do it once you are at the gates of heaven.

I encourage you today to make Jesus your personal Savior as well as the Lord of your life. It is easy to accept Him as Savior but difficult to make Him a "personal" Savior. One can say, "Yes, He did come to save the world from sin." But to say, "He is mine and I am His" (a lyric from "The Best in Me" by Marvin Sapp), to have a personal, intimate, loving relationship with a being that one cannot even see, hear, or touch, takes an incredible amount of faith. There will be an invitation at the end of the book to receive Jesus into your heart, or you can do it right now—the choice is yours.

To make Jesus the Lord over one's life requires faith and a lifetime walk filled with God's grace, which we will discuss in a later chapter. Let's continue on to Chapter 2 and read more about that amazing Savior, our only intercessor.

CHAPTER 2

There Is Only One Way

Growing up in the Catholic religion, I prayed to the Virgin Mary, the Blessed Mother of our Lord, Jesus, as well as some of the saints of the Bible. My favorite was St. Jude, who I learned while growing up is the patron saint of the helpless and the depressed. My parents had statues of the holy family (Joseph, Mary, and Jesus), as well as other saints, in the house. I didn't think anything of this practice prior to my salvation, but years later, I now refer to the saints to whom I prayed as idols because I was praying to and relying on *them* to answer my prayers, not solely God through the intercession of His Son, our Savior, Jesus Christ. This may sound harsh to many who are reading this, but that was the conviction that the Lord gave me a few years into my walk with Him. Let me share some experiences that I had along my journey that will explain why I am declaring this, which is not my opinion but biblical truth.

My first encounter with this truth occurred in the workplace. My supervisor at the time, who is now my spiritual sister (her parents brought me to the Lord), noticed that I was wearing my St. Jude medallion. Another coworker and I, who were of Catholic upbringing, were talking about the saint and how he is "in charge of" helping the depressed and the "down and out." My supervisor, who was a Christian, was not and still is not the preachy type, nor was she the nosey type who would pry into people's conversations. But on this day, she felt led to join in the conversation with the purpose of correcting what we were saying from a biblical perspective, and she did so with lots of mercy (one of her main spiritual gifts, to be discussed in Chapter 3). Her parents were raised as Roman Catholics, so she had a foundation in their denominational beliefs. I cannot remember her exact words because it was so long ago, but the bottom line was that by saying St. Jude is in charge of something or is the one we go to when we are depressed, we were basically saying that God cannot handle it all, which contradicts the Bible. I did not argue; I let that statement marinate in my mind until years later, after I was born again. Little by little, I started to confront others about what the Lord says about intercessors other than Jesus. I usually add my own twist to each explanation, keeping it practical, yet biblical, which I will share in a moment. If God gives saints certain jurisdictions (for example, St. Jude's having authority over the depressed and the helpless), then there would be no need for God to be the one we go to when we are in need. This is a contradiction of the Bible, and that is the message that I strive to convey.

Before I go any further, I must emphasize that I do not want any of my friends or family members who still practice Catholicism (or any other religion that adheres to a similar doctrine) to think that my mission in this book is to bash one denomination or belief system. That is not the case. In fact, some of my family members who serve in the Catholic Church have actually given their hearts to Christ and have that special walk with Him. I grew up in the Catholic Church, and I am very grateful for the foundation that it gave me. Twelve years of education in the Catholic school system were a blessing, and they paved the way for me as well as gave me the roots that I needed to fully receive Christ and build an even more intimate relationship with Him as a born-again Christian. The reason that I am bringing up these points is that I want everyone who is reading this book to know that there really is *no other way* to get to the Father except through His Son, and it is the best relationship that you will ever have on earth and later in heaven. That is why we pray to the Father in the name of Jesus, not in the name of any other saint or being. With the Father and you in deep relationship, the Son in the middle, and the Holy Spirit coaching you through the process, you can't go wrong with this winning combination.

My mother used to wear a medallion with an image of Mary, Jesus' mother, on a necklace. One day, I asked her why she was wearing it, and she said that Mary is the one who intercedes for us to Jesus and that Jesus cannot refuse any requests that come from his mom. I did not have any Scriptures to refer to in order to correct this reasoning. (I was a Christian but not as well versed in the Word as I am now.) But I did say to Mama Cruz, "Why would you need to go to the mother if you already know the Son?" I understood why my mom thought this way, because that is what I learned in school. I remember my fourth-grade teacher telling us one day during religion class that there is nothing that the Son can refuse the Blessed Mother. But if we practice in this fashion, which is not biblically based, it would be like having a relationship with someone and then not being confident that they would do what they said they were going to do; to mitigate that lack of trust, we would ask the person's mom to ask her child on our behalf, to remind Him or her of our petition. In essence, if we practice this way, we are really not trusting in God to do what we ask of Him. Or we tend to believe, as my very worrisome and nervous Italian-Jewish mother used to think, that the Son can't refuse the mom's request, which makes me think of that famous quote that Don Corleone says in *The Godfather:* "I'm gonna make him an offer that he can't refuse." So if Jesus does not intend to bless us or answer us regarding a certain area of our lives, do we think that He will do so because His mother asked for that petition on our behalf? Will Mary make God (God and Jesus being one) change His mind about something or make Him move faster on a request? I love my mom with all my heart and love the "mom of all moms," Mary, who is a woman to be loved and respected because she was chosen to birth our Savior. However, I would not bypass the Lord and ask his mom to put in a good word for me. Along with the free gift of salvation comes a direct line to the Father, Son, and Holy Spirit. All we have to do is call.

My grandmother also wears the same medallion on her neck, but if someone were to ask her why, she wouldn't give an answer. She was taught by her parents to be a devout Catholic, yet she doesn't know how to articulate what the religion represents. However, one day, she and I were watching Dr. Charles Stanley's television program (*In Touch Ministries*), and he asked his congregation, "Who is your best friend?" My grandmother responded to the question without hesitation and with an answer that surprised me: "God." I was shocked that she didn't say the Blessed Mother, my grandfather's name, my mother's name, or the name of her favorite sibling. She said God was her best friend, which gave me confidence that she really knew, deep down, that God was the only one in whom she could trust, putting aside all of the other saints, rituals, and people in whom she may have put her trust for ninety-five years.

My father wears a St. Lazarus medallion on his necklace. His own father used to love St. Lazarus; it was his favorite of all the saints. One day, after Papa Cruz expressed to me that he had a relationship with God (which I was excited to hear), I asked him why he was wearing the medallion. He answered, "Well, Lazarus was Jesus' friend." So I asked, "So, then why don't you wear a cross to represent Jesus and not one of his friends?" I did not get a response, and I did not feel led to continue the conversation. Sometimes the Holy Spirit (whom we will discuss in Chapter 3) allows us to engage in certain conversations in order to plant some seeds, and then years later, those seeds get watered and we get to later reap a harvest. My father still wears his St. Lazarus medallion, and I will not argue about it, but I pray that the Lord will tug at his heart (as the medallion is worn so close to his heart) and prompt him to trade it in to wear something that more closely represents his relationship with Jesus, not a *friend* of Jesus. And, because our family name is Cruz, which is Spanish for "cross," I would love to see him wear a cross to represent our "namesake"! In actuality, we are all friends of God when we embark on that special relationship with Jesus, so we need to simply cut out the middle men and go straight to our best friend, the "one that sticks closer than a brother" (Prov. 18:24 NIV). I know my father has given His heart to the Lord and has that personal, yet private, relationship with Christ, so it is my prayer that in growing that relationship more and more each day, he will yearn for more depth in that walk and remove all other distractions that may stand in the way. Granted, I had my favorite saint growing up, St. Jude, and now I love the readings of the apostle Paul; he is my new "favorite" of the disciples. Despite all that, my prayers, my heart, and my trust are in the Lord and the Lord alone, through His son, Jesus, my intercessor. Even my main man, Paul, does not come before or beside Jesus.

My spiritual daughter, whom I led to Christ a few years ago, sometimes wears the same St. Lazarus medallion on her necklace. She and I were having lunch one day, and I cannot recall how the conversation got started, but I asked her why she was wearing it. (Please understand me—I am not looking to judge or go around being "the medallion police," but I simply want to plant a seed as well as explain how God is grieved when we put our trust in others before or beside Him, as mentioned in the previous chapter, or wear an adornment that represents a figure other than Him.) She told me that her mom had given it to her for protection. I didn't really know how to explain how Jesus feels when He sees us trusting in other beings for our protection and intercession to the Father, so I thought to relate it to her relationship with her boyfriend, who is now her husband. I said, and I paraphrase, "How would your boyfriend feel if you went to another man for help and did not call upon him? I am sure he would feel hurt and betrayed, almost cheated on, as if his girl were putting her trust in another and did not care about him. Maybe he would think that she did not believe he could handle the task so she sought another who she thought could help. In the same way, we are cheating on God when we believe that one of the saints can do it better." We both laughed when I said this, but there is some truth to that funny yet insightful explanation. How does the Lord feel when He, the being that created us and knew us before we were in our mothers' wombs (Jer. 1:5), who knows every hair on our heads (Luke 12:7) and has a plan and purpose for our lives (Jer. 29:11), has to play second fiddle to another? Cheated, slighted, passed over, used—that is how I believe He feels! But understand that God is a forgiving God, a merciful God, who wants us to simply come to Him for *everything*. Remember the following saying whenever you want to call up anyone else before or beside our Blessed Father, Son, and Counselor: He wants to be our one and only, not one of many!

Let's discuss the word saint for a moment, for clarification purposes. The Bible refers to a saint as someone who has received Christ as his or her personal Savior. It is stated in the New Testament, "To the church of God in Corinth, to those sanctified in Christ Jesus and called to be his holy people, together with all those everywhere who call on the name of our Lord Jesus Christ—their Lord and ours:" (1 Cor 1:2 NIV). Saints are set apart by God to be sanctified, or made holy. Saints are people who have been saved by grace; their souls have been cleansed, but because they are in human bodies, they can be prone to sin again. The only difference between a saint and a sinner is that a saint is convicted by the Holy Spirit when he or she commits a sin. Once fellowship is restored with God through Jesus, saints are picked back up after they fall and dusted off, and then they are ready to start walking again with the Lord.

Saints constitute the body of Christ, and they intercede in prayer to the Lord on behalf of others, in the name of Jesus. Some Christian denominations teach that saints are those who have been given a special ranking in heaven based on what they have done on earth. Biblically speaking, however, all those who receive Christ are considered saints in the Christian faith. The apostles; Mary, Jesus' mother; Mary Magdalene; and all of the prophets and godly men and women who received God's Son are saints, but so are all those who call upon the name of the Lord to be saved. So you can call me Saint Helene!

Certain Christian denominations believe that saints have powers and that we are to call upon them for protection. Again, I feel led to state that my goal in writing this chapter is not to offend anyone's belief system, nor to criticize, but to correct according to God's Word (the Bible). If we are calling upon another or several saints, gods, beings, deities, and so on for our "protection, direction, correction, or affection," then what are we saying about God? Are we putting our whole trust in God? Do we believe that God is too busy for us, that we have to have others handle our issues because he cannot get to us due to a tight schedule? Or do we think that we are too unimportant or insignificant for God to want to hear from us, that we are not worthy to speak with Him directly? The Bible states throughout the two Testaments that God is omnipotent, omnipresent, and sovereign—meaning that He is all-powerful and all-knowing, being everywhere at all times, and is in charge of all of heaven and earth. Those are difficult concepts for us humans to grasp, but that is where faith comes in. And "faith is the substance of things hoped for, the evidence of things not seen" (Heb. 11:1 KJV). God *always* has time for His children, He knows exactly what is happening at every second, He is everywhere, and He rules everything, so busyness is not an issue for Him. By praying to others for our intercession, we are going through a mediator when, instead, we need to go directly to the source. I love it that I can speak to Him through Jesus, who in actuality is really God (that three-in-one package that I mentioned in Chapter 1).

It took me a long time to cut the middle men out of the picture. For years, even after I got saved, I dabbled in idolatry. I would pray to certain saints and even incorporate rituals from other religions that were non-Judeo-Christian in nature into my Christian walk, doing what I call "mixing and matching" my faith. I was eclectic in the construction of my belief system. I am speaking on this issue because the Lord delivered me from it and I want to shed light on those who still hold onto beliefs and practices that are contradictory to the Bible. Let me share how "all over the place" I was and how God was so patient, waiting for me to just give Him everything.

One Christmas morning in the mid-1990s, I opened my gifts with the family. Some of the gifts that I received had been on my wish list. I received a Star of David pendant (a symbol of Judaism, which I requested because my grandfather was Jewish and I wanted to get in touch with my roots). Also, I asked for my very own St. Lazarus medallion so I could be "in sync" with my dad (the same medallion about which I questioned Papa Cruz and my spiritual daughter years later). During the same holiday gift exchange, I gave my sister a book written by the Dalai Lama because I was intrigued by Buddhism, something that I thought would bring her peace because she was in a rough patch in her life at the time. Prior to becoming saved, I had attended a few Buddhist chanting sessions and had also attended "channeling" parties given by people in my friend's circle of friends, who were into Shamanism, a Native American practice. In addition, I was learning more about Santeria, which is an Afro-Caribbean "religion of the saints," and I had a close relationship with a family who had practiced it for generations. I read horoscopes and was intrigued with the Chinese zodiac; two Chinese families are close to my family, and after they shared their beliefs with us, I started to adopt some of their practices at one point. I was born in the Year of the Dog, so I was learning more about what that means in conjunction with my astrological sign, Aries. Now, I simply say that my sign is the "sign of the cross—Father, Son, and Holy Spirit!" And, this was all happening at a time where I was beginning my fascination with Islam, which lasted a few years after I saw Spike Lee's movie *Malcolm X*. In the midst of all of this eclectic, yet confusing, flow of practices, I was very depressed, very moody, and always felt a sense of aggression. I kept searching for the one practice that would really make me feel peaceful, and nothing would do. In the meantime, as I mentioned in the introduction, God was lining up Christians for me to meet along my path. Although I found Christianity to be filled with rules and regulations and Christians to be regimented, there was a peace and a joy that filled the hearts of the Christians who were put on my path. I was gravitating to that solid, steady, and godly foundation, little by little.

There is a danger in mixing and matching. If you start believing that other practices are on the "same page" with and affirm the power that Jesus Christ possesses, then you start becoming confused, deceived, misled and also defiled ("made dirty"). I know this may sound dramatic, but let me explain what I mean by these terms. When you open the door to other beliefs that contradict the Word of God, you allow Satan in the door, believe it or not. I am sure that right now you are thinking, *So what are you saying—that what I'm doing is evil?* Unfortunately, the answer is yes. Although your intentions may not be evil, you are letting the Devil find a foothold (an "entrance"), even a stronghold (a "heavy grip"), on your life by allowing you to pervert (twist) your foundation. Pretty soon, if you mix belief systems together, you will start to become unclear as to what the truth really is. And the truth will be distorted to the point of being lost underneath all of the other stuff. Remember that "No man can serve two masters: for either he will hate the one, and love the other; or else he will hold to the one, and despise the other. Ye cannot serve God and mammon" (Matt. 6:24 KJV). This Scripture is usually quoted in lessons pertaining to the love of God and money; however, it can easily relate to choosing other pathways to heaven. It is not possible to walk on two or more roads at the same time, so how can anyone practice several faiths and be committed to just one? If you serve two (or more) ways, you are going to start favoring one over the other. And chances are that you will start to favor and eventually cling to the faith or practice that makes you feel the best in the here and now, which may not necessarily be God's truth. One of Satan's (our enemy, who we will discuss in more detail in later chapters) sharpest tools is to distract and to pervert truth. If Satan sees that we are allowing other so-called truths into our lives, he looks for an opening to get in on the act and see how he can get us away from the perfect will of God in our lives. That is Satan's goal—to move us away from the plan that God has for each and every one of us. Matthew 7:13–14 (NIV) warns us about us going down a narrow path and choosing one that is not too wide, allowing other practices into our belief system. "Enter through the narrow gate. For wide is the gate and broad is the road that leads to destruction, and many enter through it.

But small is the gate and narrow the road that leads to life and only a few find it." So when people say that I am narrow-minded because I am a born-again Christian, I can quote this Scripture and gladly agree!

In addition to idolatry, the Bible is very clear about occult (magical) practices, which are such a part of our mainstream culture today. The Word clearly states in Deuteronomy 18:9–14 (NIV),

> When you enter the land the LORD your God is giving you, do not learn to imitate the detestable ways of the nations there. Let no one be found among you who sacrifices their son or daughter in the fire, who practices divination or sorcery, interprets omens, engages in witchcraft, or casts spells, or who is a medium or spiritist or who consults the dead. Anyone who does these things is detestable to the LORD; because of these same detestable practices the LORD your God will drive out those nations before you. You must be blameless before the LORD your God. The nations you will dispossess listen to those who practice sorcery or divination. But as for you, the LORD your God has not permitted you to do so.

I truly believe that my fascination with all of these religious practices as well as other "occult" practices were so attractive to me because God was getting me ready to receive Him, and most distractions come when a breakthrough is around the corner. The Enemy wants to throw some curveballs and tempt us with things that falsely promise peace, joy, hope, righteousness, freedom, etc.—but what he delivers are lies. The last thing Satan wanted was for me to go to Christ and, thirteen years later, write a book about walking with Christ in love, encouraging all readers to drink the true "cup of life." The goal of my writing this book is to bring awareness of peace, grace, and mercy and, most important, to evangelize to those who don't know, or don't want to know, God's own Son.

Jesus sits at the right hand of the Father, interceding on behalf of His brothers and sisters. As Timothy writes in his first book, second chapter, fifth verse (NIV): "For there is one God and one mediator between God and men, the man Christ Jesus."

Jesus is the only means to the Father. Being at God's side, He has God's ear (also His heart). The amazing thing about Jesus is that He *is* God, brought to earth in human form, but is one with the Lord. His mission on earth has been accomplished; He was resurrected and is in heaven now but still lives today.

In the next chapter, we will be discussing the role of the Holy Spirit, who is one with God the Father and Jesus the Son. He is the Counselor to those who call upon the name of the Lord and who are saved. The Holy Spirit is a guiding force in every believer's life; I cannot wait to share with you how the Holy Spirit shows up and how powerful He is! Before we end this chapter, I urge you to stop what you are doing and take a moment to digest what has been presented in these two chapters because it is information that will change your life if you have not yet accepted Christ. Also, if you have been dabbling in other practices or operating in religions that are idolatrous in nature, please take a moment to get alone with the Lord and ask Him to forgive you for seeking your help and guidance elsewhere. He wants to be the only one that you cling to, and He will welcome you with open arms to an intimate relationship with Him that doesn't require that you involve any beings or practices other than the intercessor—Jesus Himself.

And, if you are already a follower of Jesus, the biblical references will be a reaffirmation to you, and I am sure you will be able to relate to some of the stories that I have shared. Thank you for reading and allowing me to "break it down" in a personal way. There is nothing more personal than communicating with the Lord, and for the Lord, in the name of Jesus.

CHAPTER 3

The Counselor Is In

In the fourteenth chapter of the Gospel of John, Jesus sets the stage for the apostles by preparing them for His departure from the earth. But He does not leave them empty-handed. In verses 16 and 17 (NIV), Jesus promises them the following: "And I will ask the Father, and He will give you another Counselor to be with you forever—the Spirit of truth. The world cannot accept Him, because it neither sees Him nor knows Him. But you know Him for He lives with you and will be in you." Jesus goes on to explain in verse 26 (NIV), "But the Counselor, the Holy Spirit, whom the Father will send in my name, will teach you all things and will remind you of everything I have said to you." And, after His death, Jesus appeared to His disciples and said in John 20:22 (NIV), "Receive the Holy Spirit."

The Holy Spirit, as I previously wrote, is the third person of the Trinity, the three-in-one package to which I have referred. The Holy Spirit is called the Counselor and, sometimes, the Comforter. I like to call Him the Compass because He is the one who directs us in our lives and shows us the way. His main purpose is to live and work in the mind, soul, and heart of every person who is truly born again. I say *truly* because many have prayed a prayer of surrender to Christ but have not really surrendered in their hearts—their prayers may have been all lip-service. As I stated in Chapter 1, Jesus is the only way, so we have to remember "that if you confess with your mouth, 'Jesus is Lord,' and believe in your heart that God raised Him from the dead, you will be saved" (Rom. 10:9 NIV). Therefore, once you do this, your soul will be cleansed with the blood of Jesus, you will have the Lord in your heart, and the Holy Spirit will immediately come to dwell inside of you from that point of conversion for all eternity. Only those who declare what is written in Romans 10:9 will have the power of the Holy Spirit inside of them.

However, there is a difference between having the Holy Spirit coming to take up residence in your heart, which happens the moment that you come to the cross and accept Christ, and being baptized by the Holy Spirit. The perfect example of being baptized by, or filled with, the Holy Spirit was when the apostles were gathered together for the feast of Pentecost. This was captured in Acts 2:1–4 (AMP).

> And when the day of Pentecost had fully come, they were all assembled together in one place, when suddenly there came a sound from heaven like the rushing of a violent tempest blast, and it filled the whole house in which they were sitting. And there appeared to them tongues resembling fire, which were separated and distributed and which settled on each one of them. And they were all filled (diffused throughout their souls) with the Holy Spirit and began to speak in other (different, foreign) languages (tongues), as the Spirit kept giving them clear and loud expression [in each tongue in appropriate words].

This incredible movement of the Holy Spirit enabled the apostles to go out and minister to the masses in the languages of the nations to which they were sent and to be "anointed" by the Holy Spirit (having that special "presence of the Lord" on each and every one of them). After that, the apostles ministered to and evangelized to thousands. That was an amazing outpouring of the Holy Spirit that happened not only in Bible times but in our time today as well. The Holy Spirit is alive and well in us and shows up when we call upon the name of the Lord for counsel, direction, healing, change, and so on.

The Holy Spirit is also known as the Helper, a role He fills especially when we don't know what to pray for or how to pray. In Romans 8:26–27 (NIV), we read the following: "In the same way, the Spirit helps us in our weakness. We do not know what we ought to pray for, but the Spirit Himself intercedes for us through wordless groans. And He who searches our hearts knows the mind of the Spirit because the Spirit intercedes for God's people in accordance with the will of God." There have been many times when I was in prayer and just didn't know how to pray for a particular petition or was so tired of praying about a situation and was beginning to believe that I had to change the way I was praying in order to get a breakthrough. Sometimes I get so overwhelmed with all that is coming against me, and other times I have been praying about something for so long that I don't know how to pray about that particular need any longer. These are the prayer times where I have to be alone with the Lord and wait on Him to speak to me. The Holy Spirit will be the outlet—or the spark plug, so to speak—to stir up our prayers and allow us to utter the right words to speak to the Lord and present our requests. It is very difficult for me to wait on the Lord to speak because I am a talker and want to tell the Lord everything that is pressing on my heart. I usually begin my prayer time with the Lord very early in the morning (in the wee hours of the A.M., as I like to call it), and I bring all of my anxieties to Him almost in machine-gun fashion, talking a mile a minute just to rid my spirit of the anxiety that I may be carrying over from the previous day. I laugh because I tend to retreat from people who talk to me in that same fashion, yet I am come at God first thing in the morning like a gangbuster! It is a beautiful thing that the Lord is full of mercy and grace and totally understands His daughter, for I am so eager to clear my head and my heart of the junk that I sometimes bulldoze Him. I am just so grateful that I can go to the throne at any time of day, giving Him all my tales of woe. As 1 Peter 5:7 (NIV) says, "Cast all your anxiety on him because he cares for you." Then, I can get my head and heart clear so that the Holy Spirit can show me what He needs me to do that day.

However, there are days when I am not in panic mode, when I wake up and can "be still and know that He is God" (Ps. 46:10 NIV). That is the best time for the Holy Spirit to prompt me to ask for the things that are in alignment with the perfect will of God. The Holy Spirit, being the third member of the greatest trio that ever existed, knows what pleases the Father and Son, so it is best to wait on Him, call upon the presence of the Holy Spirit, and allow Him to speak on your behalf. I can remember several times when my prayer times were so anointed by the Holy Spirit that I felt His presence with fervor. Granted, every time I pray, the Holy Spirit is right there alongside God and Jesus, but there are special times when, mostly in prayer with other saints, the Holy

Spirit simply "falls" on us and moves our prayer time to another level. Sometimes the Holy Spirit does literally fall on believers and knocks them to the ground. That hasn't happened to me yet but has to people I know very well. The presence of Holy Spirit is so strong that there may be instances of its manifestation other than just people falling out. Let's talk about this next.

The Holy Spirit is also known in the New Testament simply as Spirit, and that spirit manifests, or shows itself strongly, in a number of ways through each believer of Jesus Christ. According to 1 Corinthians 12:4–11 (NIV), below, when we receive the Holy Spirit, God also imparts certain gifts in us that will shine through and, as I like to call it, "activate" if the Holy Spirit is working through a believer.

> There are different kinds of gifts, but the same Spirit distributes them. There are different kinds of service, but the same Lord. There are different kinds of working, but in all of them and in everyone it is the same God at work. Now to each one the manifestation of the Spirit is given for the common good. To one there is given through the Spirit a message of wisdom, to another a message of knowledge by means of the same Spirit, to another faith by the same Spirit, to another gifts of healing by that one Spirit, to another miraculous powers, to another prophecy, to another distinguishing between spirits, to another speaking in different kinds of tongues, and to still another the interpretation of tongues. All these are the work of one and the same Spirit, and he distributes them to each one, just as he determines.

We don't know exactly in which manner the Holy Spirit is going to manifest Himself, nor do we know when and where, as the Word says, but the Lord determines in what fashion the gifts will manifest themselves. There is something about a group of saints (believers, those who are saved or "born again") gathering and calling upon the name of the Lord. Chances are that the Holy Spirit will come on the scene, and God will do something special, as Matthew 18:20 (AMP) indicates: "For wherever two or three are gathered (drawn together as My followers) in (into) My name, there I AM in the midst of them." Along with the prompting of the Holy Spirit and the anointing of the saints present, there have been instances when I have given a prophetic word to another, which is a gift from the Spirit, or laid hands on a coworker or a friend and prayed for healing and watched him or her walk away without pain. I don't take the credit for these occurrences; I refer people who are not in the Lord to 1 Corinthians 12 to support what has just happened in their midst.

My strongest gifts out of the nine that are described in this Scripture are wisdom and discernment of spirits; in my own personal experience, they seem to go together. I operate in those two "gifts of manifestation" most frequently. For the most part, I tend to give counsel that is wise, pondering future consequences for myself as well as others. I am a thinker by personality type, which is something that I used to think was a negative quality. I now realize that the spiritual gift of wisdom, coupled with the tendency to be thoughtful, has been a blessing to me as well as many others. The gift of discernment has really benefited others greatly; generally speaking, I have worn my "spiritual antennae" and sensed that something (or someone) was not right or was just "off," as I like to say. This gift has kept me from dating or becoming friends with certain people who later turned out to have serious problems, from walking with people who came with ungodly spirits or bad intentions, from accepting a job that wasn't for me, and from buying a home that wasn't the right place for me to live. Also, I have learned to call out with what spirit(s) people are walking, good and evil alike. Thank you, Holy Spirit, for the gifts of wisdom and discernment!

Although God has not used me as the actual vehicle through which the Holy Spirit "shows up" to perform miracles and grant healing from serious diseases or illnesses, I have seen those two gifts manifested in my lifetime, all for the glory of God. I have healed only minor aches and pains, but God can use us for the big stuff, too, if He wants to do so. I have witnessed people in my own family and circle of friends coming out of comas, surviving heart attacks and strokes, being healed from terminal diseases, and coming out of other near-death experiences because believers were crying out and the Holy Spirit operated through someone in order to bring healing or a miracle. I have not spoken in nor have I interpreted tongues, yet I sense in my spirit when someone is going to allow the Holy Spirit to operate through them in this fashion in order to edify the body of Christ. It is very common in certain Christian denominations to have a congregation praying in tongues, just as the disciples did at Pentecost after Jesus arose from the dead.

In reference to the gifts outlined in 1 Corinthians 12, I strongly recommend that you seek the Lord to fully understand the purposes of each gift and speak with your pastor or other church leader if you are unclear as to how the Holy Spirit operates through the body of Christ as each gift is being used. It is such a blessing to witness people, or even experience for yourself, using their gifts and seeing how the Holy Spirit can show up in so many different ways. No two ways are ever the same!

The Spirit also gives us what are called motivational gifts. Romans 12:6–8 (AMP) says,

> Having gifts (faculties, talents, qualities) that differ according to the grace given us, let us use them: [He whose gift is] prophecy, [let him prophesy] according to the proportion of his faith; [He whose gift is] practical service, let him give himself to serving; he who teaches, to his teaching; He who exhorts (encourages), to his exhortation; he who contributes, let him do it in simplicity and liberality; he who gives aid and superintends, with zeal and singleness of mind; he who does acts of mercy, with genuine cheerfulness and joyful eagerness.

And, when you are serving the body of Christ in your home church, you may find that believers possess certain gifts that the Lord grants us and through which the Holy Spirit direct us in ministry, as written in Ephesians 4:11 (AMP).

> And His gifts were [varied; He Himself appointed and gave men to us] some to be apostles (special messengers), some prophets (inspired preachers and expounders), some evangelists (preachers of the Gospel, traveling missionaries), some pastors (shepherds of His flock) and teachers.

Motivational gifts are exactly what the name implies. Once we are born again, the Holy Spirit deposits certain gifts in us, and no two Christians have the same combination of gifts; we are all unique. Typically, each believer is given one or more of the seven motivational gifts that move him or her to act in a certain way. For example, one of my strongest gifts is exhortation, or encouragement, as it is referred to in many versions of the Bible. My immediate response when dealing with the body of Christ—and nonbelievers, for that matter—is to impart a word of encouragement. My primary interest is in motivating others to come up higher, to see the "brighter side" of a situation, and to walk away laughing even though they originally came to me crying. It moves my spirit to be a support to my brothers and sisters. However, I also have the gift of prophecy, which calls for a person to be the "eyes" of the church, being able to give warnings or to know when someone is speaking or acting contrary to the Word of God. In the past, I have stifled this gift, especially when people were engaging in practices that were contrary to the Bible, taking a portion of Scripture and perverting it to suit their needs. Now, I am more "in tune" with this gift, speaking (mostly writing) more boldly, giving correction and warning when appropriate or when I discern that a person is open to hearing God's truth.

I love to be around brothers and sisters who possess motivational gifts in which I am deficient, for I am not the strongest in the areas of mercy and leadership. So when I encounter someone who demonstrates these gifts, I get motivated by their motivational gifts! Of course, I love to be around those who like to encourage because everyone needs a little boost every now and then, especially those who "pour out" a lot, for their cups sometimes run empty and need to be replenished. That happens to me quite a bit; there are days that I have lots of support to give, whether it is writing e-mails or texts or talking to people in person or on the telephone. And then there are days when I feel like I am at less than zero on the speedometer and need to be refueled. God always gives you what you need, though, which is a blessing.

Ministerial gifts, as cited in Ephesians 4:11, lead each believer into the area of ministry in which they will be most gifted. Most likely, the Lord will allow your motivational gifts to align with where you are in ministry. The Amplified version of Ephesians 4:11 does a great job in defining those five main areas. When I first came to Christ Tabernacle, I wondered about those who intercede in prayer for others, standing in the gap in prayer (prayer intercessors or warriors), as well as those who are called to worship (musicians and singers). I didn't see those amazing gifts mentioned in this portion of Scripture, but they are two main areas of ministry. But in reading the Word, I came to realize that *all* of God's children in the body of Christ are sanctioned to praise and worship Him, as well as to pray to Him. (This is all part of our intimate walk with the Lord.) Some people have a natural talent for singing and playing musical instruments, and they willingly accept that calling by blessing us with their amazing voices and instrument playing for the Lord.

I was in the choir in elementary school. I have a decent voice, though I will never be a soloist, and I love to listen to praise and worship music. However, as much as I would love to join my fellow brothers and sisters in my church's choir, I *know* that I am not called to do minister in that fashion. My true callings are to pray, encourage, teach, and evangelize, and those are the ways that God wants me to feed His sheep. That is where I have been and will continue to be the most effective—and anointed. I don't want to join the choir and then see that there will be no anointing, no grace, and no peace, to see the whole thing, as I like to say, "go totally flat." So this is a word to those who are trying to discover God's calling in ministry for them. A helpful hint is that if you are not sensing God's presence in something or if there is absolutely no peace when you are doing it, chances are that what you are doing is not what God wants for you in terms of serving His people.

A word to prayer warriors out there—you have been a tremendous blessing in my life and to all people inside and outside of the body of Christ. It has been prophesied by several saints who possess the gift of prophecy that I am a mighty prayer warrior. At first, I didn't receive that word. I didn't believe it because, at the time, I didn't feel led to pray for others. I had to grow into the gift. Even to this day, I pray at church but don't operate in a ministry that calls for prayer (such as daily prayer bands, weekly prayer meetings, and altar calls where people give their hearts to Jesus). However, God has used me in the workplace to pray for and pray with the community. My office has served as a sanctuary on occasion, and our weekly prayer meetings have destroyed many a yoke. God saw that I needed to operate in the gift of prayer more in my secular workplace than in the church, where many of my anointed prayer warriors are already "holding down the fort" all along the watchtower.

I do believe that those who operate in one of these five categories within ministry are given a special grace and a special anointing for worship and prayer because they really need to call upon the Lord to get direction in order to direct the body of Christ. It is wise to start identifying those brothers and sisters who are gifted in these areas to make sure that they are fortified. In fact, this is true for all saints so that they will not experience ministerial burnout. Isn't it great that God has called and equipped saints, whether apostle or prophet, to give a special message to the body; pastors to lead the sheep and be accountable to the "flock" or the congregation; deacons (teachers) to facilitate the pastors by leading, teaching, praying for, counseling, and sometimes rebuking (correcting) the saints; and evangelists to preach the gospel around the world in the mission field, on TV, in books, or by taking it to the streets, schools, prisons, and so on.

Before we end this chapter, I would like to briefly discuss the fruit of the spirit that God would like to grow in us via the work of the Holy Spirit. As God grows this fruit, those who are in Christ must abandon certain desires of the flesh so they can develop this fruit, which is described in Galatians 5:19–26 (AMP).

> Now the doings (practices) of the flesh are clear (obvious): they are immorality, impurity, indecency, idolatry, sorcery, enmity, strife, jealousy, anger (ill temper), selfishness, divisions (dissensions), party spirit (factions, sects with peculiar opinions, heresies), envy, drunkenness, carousing, and the like. I warn you beforehand, just as I did previously, that those who do such things shall not inherit the kingdom of God. *But the fruit of the [Holy] Spirit [the work which His presence within accomplishes] is love, joy (gladness), peace, patience (an even temper, forbearance), kindness, goodness (benevolence), faithfulness, gentleness (meekness, humility), self-control (self-restraint, continence). Against such things there is no law* [that can bring a charge]. And those who belong to Christ Jesus (the Messiah) have crucified the flesh (the godless human nature) with its passions and appetites and desires. If we live by

the [Holy] Spirit, let us also walk by the Spirit. [If by the Holy
Spirit we have our life in God, let us go forward walking in
line, our conduct controlled by the Spirit.] Let us not become
vainglorious and self-conceited, competitive and challenging
and provoking and irritating to one another, envying and being
jealous of one another. (Emphasis added)

God will use several tactics in order to grow the fruit of the spirit. But as
you read in this Scripture and throughout Paul's epistles, we must crucify
the flesh—and there are many activities in which we may have engaged
that scream *Flesh!* The Lord has been dealing with me on three areas of
the fruit of the Spirit—peace, long-suffering (patience), and self-control.
I have come a very long way in my level of patience—God has me
waiting in many areas of my life, which we will discuss in "The Waiting
Game" chapter—but it has taken years, and yet I am still challenged from
time to time when I am short with others or not patient in situations.
In the area of peace, there have been peaks of victory but also detours
into the valley, especially because I come from a family that has tended
toward anxiety for many generations. (We'll expand upon this in the
"Trust, Obey, and Forgive" chapter.) We all have strongholds in our
families that necessitate our praying for breakthroughs, but sometimes
the best breakthrough is a gradual one, where the Holy Spirit will just
chip away at these areas and grow that fruit little by little. My biggest
struggle is with self-control; for years, I was not obedient in that area and
experienced the "pleasure principle" that psychologists refer to when
they speak about instant gratification, which, I believe, is a version of
impatience. Today, I have a handle in this area for the most part, but
every now and then I get "in the flesh," so to speak, and do something
that I should not be doing or say something with a strong tone that is
not pleasing to God. The Holy Spirit grows the fruit of the spirit in us,
and it is a process, sometimes a lifelong one, so don't be discouraged if
you struggle in certain areas. Continue to pray, receive God's grace and
mercy, and ask the Lord to speak to you about what needs to change.

In essence, it is such a blessing to have the Holy Spirit living on the
inside of us as believers so we can have that "burglar alarm," as I call
it, go off inside of us when we are out of line or out of balance. And,
without a doubt, the alarm will sound when we are acting in the flesh

and need a word of correction from the Lord. The Lord has given us this wonderful counselor and spiritual coach who will give us the pep talks that we need when we stumble, dust us off, and pick us back up to start again. God also gives us many gifts and talents upon salvation, through the power of the Holy Spirit, that will guide us daily and also equip us in ministry to serve those in need in our home churches, workplaces, families, and communities—all for His glory! So be encouraged, saints, that you have a God who is three people in one and who plays a variety of roles in our lives—Father, Savior, and Counselor!

Now that we have covered the Trinity in a nutshell (and I didn't even scratch the surface!), let us move forward to touch upon several other key Scriptures that are some of my favorites in order to make your walk with the Lord a little stronger and your burdens in the world a lot lighter. Please note that the subjects on which I am writing are in the order in which the Lord has placed them on my heart, so there may not be a flow and you may think there is no rhyme or reason to the sequence of chapter topics. I have written each chapter, as you can see, in devotional style so that you can read each chapter in one day, meditate on each topic, and digest the Scriptures.

CHAPTER 4

The Words that Jesus Taught Us

One of the most important, if not *the* most important, prayer in the Bible is featured in Matthew 6:9–13. It is a prayer that Jesus taught His disciples and the people as He was ministering to them. After this chapter, I encourage you to read Matthew, Chapters 5–7, for a better sense of what Jesus what teaching that day on the mountain. Chapter 6 contains the prayer known as the Lord's Prayer, the words that the Father gave Jesus to share with His people.

> Our Father who is in heaven, hallowed (kept holy) be Your name. Your kingdom come, Your will be done on earth as it is in heaven. Give us this day our daily bread. And forgive us our debts, as we also have forgiven (left, remitted, and let go of the debts, and have given up resentment against) our debtors. And lead (bring) us not into temptation, but deliver us from the evil one. For Yours is the kingdom and the power and the glory forever. Amen. (AMP)

I want to dissect this prayer line by line and grasp what Jesus was saying so that when you pray it, it will have a whole new meaning for you. When I did this for myself, it changed the way I prayed the prayer. I learned it many years ago as it was one of the prayers that we had to memorize and recite in school. However, I had said it so many times in my life that I never really paid attention to its depth or what I was *really* saying to our heavenly Father. So let's approach this prayer from a different perspective and take it to another level.

"Our Father, who art in Heaven, hallowed be thy name" is the opening line of the Lord's Prayer. God is our Father—Jesus' Father and yours, too! So claim it and declare it—"our father." He is our heavenly father, seated on the throne of the heavens that He created, watching over the earth that He designed. His name is *definitely* holy! So when we go to Him, we need to go as we would to royalty—with honor, praise, admiration, awe, and respect. I don't know if you are like me, but I get distracted very easily, especially when I am in "prayer mode." Hence, I am sharing this with you in so much detail because I have gone to the Lord many times but have not always given Him my full attention. It is best to pour everything into Him at that moment of intimacy because He has poured everything into you. God created the heavens and the earth and everything in both realms, including us. We would not be here if not for God, despite what evolutionists may conclude. We are His masterpieces; God doesn't create junk, so we *must* be special in His eyes. Let's meet Him in prayer in the same special way.

As you are envisioning your Father in heaven, who is holy and worthy to be praised, try to picture the world at His feet. Now, that is not to say that God is an arrogant God, stomping on the world, but His Word says that He created the world and everything in it. Also, it is written in Isaiah 66:1 (NIV), "This is what the LORD says: 'Heaven is my throne, and the earth is my footstool.'" The earth is a footstool to the Lord—wow. We are under His feet, and He *still* wants to fellowship with us! Because the Lord is in control, let us go to Him in prayer in "surrender mode," giving up our wills and our game plans to Him. This may be difficult to do if you have not had the best experience with your earthly father, creating a negative concept of "father," or if you have a hard time having a relationship with someone whom you can't literally see, feel, hear, or smell, but that is where your faith has to come into play in order to sense His presence on a spiritual level.

I am not sure if you go to the Lord on your knees, on your face, standing, or sitting. I like to go to Him in my "prayer chair," curled up in a little ball, and have my intimate moments with Him. It is a comfortable position, and it allows me to be peaceful. However, I have prayed standing up with arms extended to heaven and have been on my knees, too, depending on the urgency of the prayer request. The bottom line of this is that you go to Him; don't get caught up in the method or posture in which you do so—just go to Him!

"Your kingdom come, your will be done on earth as it is in heaven" is the second line in the prayer. His kingdom came through Jesus Christ, the Savior—through Jesus' life, crucifixion, death (which entailed defeating the Devil and burying our sins), resurrection, and ascension into heaven, where he is now seated at God's right hand. And that kingdom is going to come again when Jesus returns—exactly when, we don't know, but we do know how (read the book of Revelation in order to understand the second coming of Christ). We are waiting for Jesus to come, but we are not being still; we are busy serving Him, doing His will. We want God's will to be done here on earth, just as it is in heaven. What we want to ask is for the Lord to show us what to bind up on this earth based on what is bound up in heaven and what we need to loosen on this earth based on what is loose in heaven. As written in 1 Peter 5:8 (AMP), "Be well balanced (temperate, sober of mind), be vigilant and cautious at all times; for that enemy of yours, the devil, roams around like a lion roaring [in fierce hunger], seeking someone to seize upon and devour." The devil's mission is to "kill, steal, and destroy," but Jesus came so we can live life and live it more abundantly (John 10:10 NIV). When we go to God and pray the Lord's Prayer, we want to ask that all that is evil, every demonic spirit on this earth, be bound, or gagged and thrown back into the pit of hell, as I like to say! Then, we want what God has loosened in heaven to be loose (or free to roam) on earth—His will, His Holy Spirit, all that is good in God's eyes. We want it to engulf and permeate the earth. It is at this point of the prayer that I get specific in terms of naming the types of evil spirits I discern to be trying to dominate my life and the lives of my loved ones—spirits that need to be banished! If God is telling us that His will is going to be done on earth as it is in Heaven, then it is *not* His will to see the people in my circle or me in bondage and strife, and those spirits that would cause us to be so need to flee in the name of Jesus.

"Give us this day our daily bread" is the next line and one on which I spend a little time when I pray. We have to ask the Lord to give us what we need each day. Once, I heard a saying, and I don't know the exact source so that I can accurately quote it, but it goes something like this: "Yesterday is history, tomorrow is a mystery, but today is a gift, and that is why we call it the present." We need to treat every day as a gift from God, so precious, and not take any day for granted. It is important to be mindful and to put things in our prayers that apply to tomorrow, but it is best to pray about what God wants for you today and to spend most of your prayer time on the present. As James wrote in chapter 4, verses 13–15 (NIV),

> Come now, you who say, today or tomorrow we will go into such and such a city and spend a year there and carry on our business and make money. Yet you do not know [the least thing] about what may happen tomorrow. What is the nature of your life? You are [really] but a wisp of vapor (a puff of smoke, a mist) that is visible for a little while and then disappears [into thin air]. You ought instead to say, if the Lord is willing, we shall live and we shall do this or that [thing].

We don't know what the Lord has in store for us tomorrow, if He will even *give* us tomorrow, so we have to preface everything that we are planning or petitioning in prayer with "Lord willing" or "God willing." Chances are good that God will give you another day, but you don't know if His plan for you that day is in alignment with your prayers, so it is best to ask Him to chart your course for the day ahead. Remember, "The steps of a [good] man are directed and established by the Lord when He delights in his way [and He busies Himself with his every step]" (Ps. 37:23 AMP).

Sometimes we pray about what we want, but we need to start praying about what God *knows* we need and about the needs of others, not just our own. Know that God sees the end from the beginning. After all, He is "the Alpha and the Omega, the First and the Last, the Beginning and the End" (Rev. 22:13 NIV). He knows what lies ahead for you and can move things out of the way to enable it, just as He can put the right things, events, people, and so forth on your path. You may not even know that He spared you from danger or disaster, sometimes even death. That is why He gave Jesus the line about bread in the prayer, to say, *Lord, give us what we need today, not just the basic needs like food, water, shelter, work, and all the essentials that we need to function today but also all of the other "pieces" of bread that we may need to meet all of our spiritual, emotional, mental, social/ relational, professional/educational, financial, ministerial, familial, psychological needs as well.*

"And forgive us our trespasses, as we forgive those who trespass against us" (paraphrasing the Amplified version) is the next line in the prayer. That is a difficult line for many of us to pray. I will discuss forgiveness a little bit more in Chapter 7 because it is a struggle for Christians and non-Christians alike. Jesus died to save us from our past, present, and future sins; however, we do have to go to Him *daily*, confess our sins even though He knows what we did even before we did it, and then repent for (turn away from) those sins. By going to the Father and asking for forgiveness, you are showing Him that you want to purify your heart and also restore fellowship with Him. Along with the Lord's forgiving us of our sins, we must also forgive others who have sinned, or trespassed, against us. This is the more difficult of the two requests—it is easy for us to ask the Lord to pardon us, but when we are asked to pardon others, it can be a challenge. How can we forgive what people have done to us, especially when they may not even be sorry for what they did? Well, sometimes people do not realize what they have done to us, and we carry those grudges around, poisoning our hearts and keeping the Lord from forgiving us. Jesus told a parable, described in Matthew 18, about debt—please read it right after this chapter, if you can—and the message that I want to convey with this story was captured in the last verse (35 AMP): "So also My heavenly Father will deal with every one of you if you do not freely forgive your brother from your heart his offenses." God will not forgive us of our debts if we do not free our debtors from their offenses. Recently, my spiritual father referred me to this Scripture when I shared my heart with him and told him that I was still harboring unforgiveness in my heart toward someone very close to me. I felt so convicted by this word, but I have to admit that it is still difficult for me to let go. Sometimes I feel like a dog on a bone when it comes to holding grudges, almost like I am holding the debtors hostage for what they did to me. Let me tell you that it is a daily process for me to let go and let God handle it. I have to bring it to the Lord every day.

"And lead us not into temptation, but deliver us from the evil one" is the line that follows. In James 1:13 (AMP), it is written, "Let no one say when he is tempted, I am tempted from God; for God is incapable of being tempted by [what is] evil and He Himself tempts no one." God is not the author of temptation—that would be Satan, and sometimes our own fleshly desires and lusts take over our minds along with Satan's "antics." However, God allows us free will and, at the same time, "No temptation has overtaken you except what is common to mankind. And God is faithful; he will not let you be tempted beyond what you can bear. But when you are tempted, he will also provide a way out so that you can endure it" (1 Cor. 10:13 NIV). Our intention in declaring this part of the prayer is to say, *Father, God, I know temptations will come, especially in these last days, as we are in End Times, as the world is more decadent than it has ever been. Father, I am asking you to lead me not into such temptations and also deliver me (turn me away from, block me from) such evil should temptation be presented to me.*

"For Yours is the kingdom and the power and the glory forever, Amen" is the final line of the Lord's Prayer. This is simply saying that there is a kingdom established on this earth and below this earth, but the kingdom that the Lord has established is *the* kingdom—the one that created all and has dominion over all other kingdoms, even those that are not of a godly nature. God's kingdom has the power over all and therefore deserves glory and praise forever, for all eternity. *Amen* means, "So be it"—end of discussion. We cannot pay any heed to any other god or any other kingdom, practice, or way. Granted, we need to be mindful of the practices of those kingdoms, but as Christians, we know from where our help comes (Ps. 121), and as believers, we need to stand in the authority of the one who has dominion over us.

As I like to say, "I report to Jesus." He is my "director" and is over all others who have authority over me. God is also my primary care physician as well as my specialist for every ache and pain. I have to give Him the glory, honor, and praise that He so deserves, for He is everyone's boss, and that is the most special job in the universe. It is a job that I would not want and could never handle, but God handles it with a holy ease because He is God. With all of this being said, if God is for us, who can be against us (Rom. 8:31 NIV)?

Now when you pray the Lord's Prayer, you will see it from a different perspective. And feel free to pray that the Lord will show you what *He* wants you to get out of praying it to Him, not just what I have shared. Your experience in praying it now may produce fresh new revelations.

In the next chapter, I will continue on the subject of prayer and also how it can be a powerful tool when coupled with fasting. I pray that you were blessed by this dissection of the Lord's Prayer and that you will get into "prayer mode" as we turn the page to Chapter 5.

CHAPTER 5

"The Dynamic Duo": Prayer and Fasting

Prayer is communication with the Lord. Fasting is sacrificing something in order to hear God's voice more clearly, without distraction of that particular thing from which you are fasting. Prayer and fasting go together, as the title of this chapter states; they are "The Dynamic Duo" (as quoted from the 1960s show *Batman*) in our relationship with the Lord. You cannot have an effective fasting period without conversation with the Lord. Prayer between the Lord and us is essential in the lives of believers. In addition, we are charged with praying for our needs as well as those of others. Timothy writes in his first letter, second chapter, verses 1–4 (AMP),

> First of all, then, I admonish and urge that petitions, prayers, intercessions, and thanksgivings be offered on behalf of all men, for kings and all who are in positions of authority or high responsibility, that [outwardly] we may pass a quiet and undisturbed life [and inwardly] a peaceable one in all godliness and reverence and seriousness in every way. For such [praying] is good and right, and [it is] pleasing and acceptable to God our Savior, who wishes all men to be saved and [increasingly] to perceive and recognize and discern and know precisely and correctly the [divine] Truth.

And, as James wrote in his second chapter, verse 16 (AMP), "Confess to one another therefore your faults (your slips, your false steps, your offenses, your sins) and pray [also] for one another, that you may be healed and restored [to a spiritual tone of mind and heart]. The earnest (heartfelt, continued) prayer of a righteous man makes tremendous power available [dynamic in its working]."

We will first talk about prayer and then fasting, as well as how effective both of them are in the lives of followers of Christ. The very first prayer that Jesus taught us was on the mountain (see Chapter 4), and it is still the most often recited prayer by Christians today. It is a prayer that is straight from the Word of God, a directive given to Jesus by God to share with us, and we must cherish it. However, prayer, as I defined in the first paragraph, is communication with God, which means that it is not necessarily something that is memorized from the Word and then recited, sometimes without feeling or meaning. I was taught the Our Father prayer, the Hail Mary, the Profession of Faith (which is part of the Catholic Mass), and the Prayer of St. Francis of Assisi as a young girl and would recite them. I can still recite them to this day! Later, as a born-again Christian, I would pray the Prayer of Jabez, which we will talk about toward the end of the book. Growing up, I never really learned how to speak to the Lord outside of these already-written and established prayers. Over the years, I learned that if I wanted to have an intimate, in-depth relationship with the Lord and wanted it to flourish, I needed to go to Him with my words, what is on my heart and mind. You need to talk to Him in your own words, in addition to the Lord's Prayer and anything biblical that you feel on your heart that you want to declare to Him, not just recite. Stormie Omartian has authored several books on prayer; the first one in the series was *The Power of a Praying Woman* (Harvest House Publishers, 2002), and other books followed (*The Power of a Praying Man, The Power of a Praying Wife/Husband,* and *The Power of a Praying Mother/Father*). I strongly recommend that you pick up one or all of her books because she has been given the anointing by the Holy Spirit to speak on prayer for the many different roles that we play in our lives. These books will definitely facilitate your journey in terms of understanding the depth and the power of prayer.

Second Timothy 1:3 says, "I thank God whom I worship with a pure conscience, in the spirit of my fathers, when without ceasing I remember you night and day in my prayers." Like Timothy, we also need to pray, and pray without ceasing. That does not mean that we have to repeat the same petitions over and over during each prayer time. We have to trust that the Lord heard us the first time. After all, God is our Father, and He wants us to trust that He hears us and will provide. He may not provide when we want or even how we want it, but He does it on His schedule, in His fashion. However, if something is on our hearts and we have not seen it come to pass, we can bring it to Him again and share how heavy it is for us so that He can grant us peace and reassurance that He is working out all of the details. Sometimes we can't see that anything is happening yet, and that can be very discouraging. I have to admit that sometimes I get a little obsessive when I pray, and it is as though I am asking God a million times about the same stuff. I say to Him, "God, you must be so annoyed with me!" God wants us to come to Him with expectancy, knowing that He will produce what we need. As Philippians 4:6 (AMP) states, "Do not fret or have any anxiety about anything, but in every circumstance and in everything, by prayer and petition (definite requests), with thanksgiving, continue to make your wants known to God." You have to bring *everything* to the Lord. I bring what people, even Christian folks, may perceive as the pettiest things to Him. But if He is my heavenly Father and He knows my beginning from my end, I want to bring it all to Him.

For example, I ask Him to order my steps each day—to whom I need to speak, what I need to say (or not say), what I should wear, where I need to be, how much money I should spend, and so on. I have even asked the Lord to change my plans for the day to bring me into alignment with what He wants me to do that day. Also, I have an intestinal condition, so I even ask for God to keep my stomach calm and give me wisdom regarding what I should eat, how much I should eat of it, and at what times of the day I should be eating it. For example, whenever I have a major presentation, I pray about what I eat before and after I speak so that I do not aggravate my intestines. God is interested in every aspect, every detail, of our lives, even the activities of our digestive and excretory systems! Why wouldn't He be? God knew of my stomach issues before I ever had them, and He allowed me to have them so that I could be more mindful of and wiser about my food selections, as well as the level of my dependency in coming to Him and trusting Him with my discomfort in that area of my life. It is awesome how God takes something intrusive and makes something good come out of it, for I now go to Him and talk to Him about my meal plan for each day.

The following is a group of Scriptures (all from the Amplified Bible) that stress that God hears our prayers and does answer them. It is good to start holding onto these, especially when you feel like you are being a pest to God or that God has given up on your requests.

Micah 7:7—"But as for me, I will look to the Lord and confident in Him I will keep watch; I will wait with hope and expectancy for the God of my salvation; my God will hear me."

Matthew 7:7–8—"Keep on asking and it will be given you; keep on seeking and you will find; keep on knocking [reverently] and [the door] will be opened to you. For everyone who keeps on asking receives; and he who keeps on seeking finds; and to him who keeps on knocking, [the door] will be opened."

Matthew 21:22—"And whatever you ask for in prayer, having faith and [really] believing, you will receive."

Mark 11:22–25—"And Jesus, replying, said to them, have faith in God [constantly]. Truly I tell you, whoever says to this mountain, Be lifted up and thrown into the sea! and does not doubt at all in his heart but believes that what he says will take place; it will be done for him. For this reason I am telling you, whatever you ask for in prayer, believe (trust and be confident) that it is granted to you, and you will [get it]. And whenever you stand praying, if you have anything against anyone, forgive him and let it drop (leave it, let it go), in order that your Father who is in heaven may also forgive you your [own] failings and shortcomings and let them drop."

1 John 5:14–15—"And this is the confidence (the assurance, the privilege of boldness) which we have in Him: [we are sure] that if we ask anything (make any request) according to His will (in agreement with His own plan), He listens to and hears us. And if (since) we [positively] know that He listens to us in whatever we ask, we also know [with settled and absolute knowledge] that we have [granted us as our present possessions] the requests made of Him."

Fasting is abstaining from food (or a certain type of food) or even refraining from any activity that you hold very near and dear to your heart in order to really seek God in prayer and also seek His direction on issues. Fasting is also a time of petitioning the Lord while you are abstaining from whatever you have decided to surrender during the fasting period in order to break the yoke of bondage off of yourself or another individual. Fasting and prayer go together, and I believe that fasting cannot be effective unless you are in prayer—in communication and in one accord with the Lord. While you are fasting, you are seeking the Lord's direction on an issue, petitioning Him to break strongholds (anything that has a "strong hold" on you or someone else), and praying for the salvation of family and friends. As Isaiah wrote in chapter 58, verse 6 (NIV), "Is not this the fast that I have chosen: to loose the bonds of wickedness, to undo the bands of the yoke, to let the oppressed go free, and that you break every enslaving yoke?"

There is a great book written by Jentezen Franklin entitled *Fasting* (Strang Book Group, 2009) that I highly recommend reading in order to understand the ins and outs of fasting. Pastor Franklin shares about the twenty-one-day fast that his congregation does corporately every January to ring in the new year and give the Lord the "first fruits" of the year by starting out seeking Him in fasting and prayer. His book is filled with testimonies of many of the breakthroughs of his congregation, how God delivered people from addictions, led people to become saved, and brought people clarity and direction on upcoming decisions that they had to make. It is definitely a must-read and the first book on fasting that comes to my mind when I'm making recommendations to others. In the book, Franklin discusses the different types of fasts one can participate in. The most popular one for his church—and many others, including mine—is what is called the Daniel Fast, which is based on the Book of Daniel in the Bible (Chapter 10). It is a twenty-one-day fast, abstaining from all meats, starches, and sweets. Basically, one eats only grains and vegetables. Of course, there are variations of this fast, but the idea is that you refrain from these particular foods that are part of our daily diets and are generally the heavier foods that may weigh us down. It is definitely a struggle for me to sacrifice chicken, pasta, rice, pizza, and desserts, and I have never lasted the entire twenty-one days (yet). In fact, I never last more than a few days, and I know that I need God's grace to get to the place where I can join my brothers and sisters in this fast next year.

And if I haven't "arrived" at the point of doing a twenty-one-day vegetable-and-grains-only fast, you know that I am nowhere near accomplishing what Jesus did in the desert for forty days and nights right before He began His three-year ministry. Jesus is the Son of God (and *is* God, simultaneously), so you are probably thinking that it was a breeze for Him to fast for this long period of time. Well, it was not. In fact, because He was gearing up to begin the most amazing ministry ever on this planet (and to go to the cross a few years later), Jesus needed to focus on the Father and hear from Him, not just in prayer but in the absence of all distractions—even food and beverages—to show God that He was really deep into His intimate time with Him. And wouldn't you know that the Devil came and tempted Him? Satan will come up anywhere and to anyone, even Jesus Christ, to distract, the ultimate goal being to kill, steal, and destroy (John 10:10). Yes, even Jesus was tempted—*especially* Jesus because Satan knew that God had the ultimate mission for Jesus to accomplish for you and me—salvation of the world. That is why Jesus needed to be still, to be alone with the Father, and to hear every word in His quiet time for those forty days. For the tasks that He was called to accomplish in His short time on earth, food could definitely wait. And, in the Judeo-Christian tradition, the number forty is symbolic of the fulfillment of prophecy. It appears throughout the Old and New Testaments, especially in the lives of Moses and Jesus; that is why Jesus was led to fast for forty days and nights. He surely needed God's direction for all that was lying ahead.

The Devil came to Jesus while He was in prayer and fasting (Luke 4:1–13) and tempted Him in the desert—not once, not twice, but three times, which shows that the Devil is relentless. And each time Satan presented Jesus with a challenge, Jesus did not fight him, nor did He give into the challenge. Jesus simply responded each time with "It is written." He didn't get in the flesh and have a showdown with the Enemy, as many of us do when we are tempted. And He did not submit because He knew no sin. Notice that Jesus knew no sin and never sinned; however, He *was* tempted because He came to earth as a man, in human flesh, and faced what we face every day. Jesus never fell into sin because God cannot sin, but He knows how weak the flesh can be.

The beautiful thing about fasting and praying together is that you are seeking the Lord, reading the Bible, and really digesting the Word so that when the Devil comes at you, you can respond just like Jesus and quote the Scriptures to shut the Devil down. That is the best defense against the Devil—knowing what God says so that we can expose the Devil's lies. Satan loves to pervert the truth, so sometimes he will approach you and speak a half-truth or rationalize sin to you so that you commit it without any conviction—but then suffer the consequences later because it just wasn't God's will for you. Because of this, we really need to know the Old and New Testaments well so that we will know when we are being deceived and fight that good fight of faith, declaring the only truth—God's truth.

Fasting allows you to have that type of experience. For example, when I am confused about decisions that I have to make or am experiencing conflict in any aspect of my life, I know I need to get into prayer but also designate a time to fast. Typically, I do a twenty-four-hour fast from all foods, keeping hydrated with water and tea. Sometimes I do this for three days in a row for consistency (not often, but sporadically). This is a "baby fast" in comparison to Jesus' and Daniel's fasting periods, but it is what I can do in this season of my walk, and God will give me the grace and direction to kick it up a notch in due time.

My fasting periods have been times for giving a word of encouragement, wisdom, revelation (truth), or prophetic warning to others whom God puts on my heart. After a fasting period, God has moved obstacles—and people—out of the way in a situation and has given clear direction, sometimes not immediately after a fast but a few days later. I have been in prayer and fasting, setting aside mealtimes to do both while I play praise and worship music. Or I may wait in silence for a word from the Lord to come into my spirit. All of a sudden, the Lord deposits the name of a person or a "burden" for someone on my heart. Sometimes while fasting, a devotional is e-mailed to me, and as I am reading it, God puts someone on my mind and directs me to forward the e-mail to that person, sometimes to someone to whom I rarely speak or e-mail.

And, on every occasion, the person will respond quickly and say, "How did you know that I needed this word today?" My response is, "I didn't know. God did, though!" Then, I get to minister to and at times pray for their needs with them. That is a blessing!

I have also learned during my fasting periods what Jesus taught His disciples in Matthew 6:16–18 (AMP).

> And whenever you are fasting, do not look gloomy and sour and dreary like the hypocrites, for they put on a dismal countenance, that their fasting may be apparent to and seen by men. Truly I say to you, they have their reward in full already. But when you fast, perfume your head and wash your face, so that your fasting may not be noticed by men but by your Father, Who sees in secret; and your Father, Who sees in secret, will reward you in the open.

I have made the mistake of mentioning to people that I am fasting, and as soon as the words are out of my mouth, I lose my peace and get agitated! I also get convicted when I disclose this because, on a few occasions, I have shared that I am fasting in order to get the kudos, be in the spotlight, or have people feel sorry for me that I wasn't able to eat! A fasting period is a very sensitive time; therefore, you have to be mindful of how you are conducting yourself, in business and in pleasure, and of what your intentions are during that period. If you are fasting and acting up, not doing right by those around you, how do you expect the Lord to speak to you or answer your plea? As Isaiah wrote in chapter 58, verses 3–5 (AMP),

> Why have we fasted, they say, and You do not see it? Why have we afflicted ourselves, and You take no knowledge [of it]? Behold [O Israel], on the day of your fast [when you should be grieving for your sins], you find profit in your business, and [instead of stopping all work, as the law implies you and your workmen should do] you extort from your hired servants a full amount of labor. [The facts are that] you fast only for strife and debate and to smite with the fist of wickedness. Fasting as you do today will not cause your voice to be heard on high. Is such a fast as

yours what I have chosen, a day for a man to humble himself with sorrow in his soul? [Is true fasting merely mechanical?] Is it only to bow down his head like a bulrush and to spread sackcloth and ashes under him [to indicate a condition of heart that he does not have]? Will you call this a fast and an acceptable day to the Lord?

In addition, you must be very careful about choosing to whom you disclose your fasting time, and check your motives in disclosing it. I have chosen a few people to keep me in prayer during that time period so I don't give in to the temptation of eating or get into any type of strife that will distract me from hearing God's Word. It is best to choose another brother or sister to fast and pray with you for the designated time period so that two or more are coming to the Lord in one accord, touching and agreeing in prayer and fasting, so that you can share revelations that the Lord has given you as well as praise reports about victories won and chains that were broken.

Members of my family are subject to many strongholds that I know will only be broken by a serious period of prayer and fasting. Pastor Franklin describes this in his book in detail, along with testimonies. These heavy-duty strongholds are only going to be lifted off by the combination of fasting and prayer—"stand-alone" prayer just won't do, and neither will haphazardly skipping a few meals for a time without spending time in prayer. When Jesus was questioned about a particular stronghold in Matthew 17, He responded, in verse 17 (AMP), "But this kind does not go out except by prayer and fasting." Certain types of bondage will break only under the power of "The Dynamic Duo."

Allow the Lord to speak to you about when to fast, for how long He wants you to fast, for what exactly He wants you to fast, and most important, why you are fasting. I pray that you will continue to pray and fast for everything that burdens your heart. If you have never prayed and fasted, may you seek the Lord's direction on how He wants you to proceed. Of course, you are going to need God's grace for anything to which He leads you. We will leave "The Dynamic Duo" chapter and begin discussing "The Twins" that will walk with you throughout your journey—Mercy and Grace!

CHAPTER 6

"The Twins": Mercy and Grace

This chapter is very special to me for two reasons. The first is that my brother in Christ and ministry partner, Derrick Jones, hosted a weekly Praise and Prayer time for over a year and extended an invitation to the saints who work at Pace to join him. This special time was called Morning Glory (like the early-morning radio program on WRKS-FM in New York) because it occurred in the early morning hours in the middle of the workweek, before the workday started. It consisted of praise and worship songs for the first half of the program and then moved into intercessory prayer and warfare prayers. Minister Jones would thank the Lord for granting us "Mercy and Grace," which he referred to as "The Twins" who walk with us daily, one over each shoulder. This is something that he heard from another source and incorporated into our weekly prayer meeting. That is so true—God grants us His grace and mercy daily. Lamentations 3:22–23 (AMP) reads, "It is because of the Lord's mercy and loving-kindness that we are not consumed, because His [tender] compassions fail not. They are new every morning; great and abundant is Your stability and faithfulness."

First, let us define the words, for I do not want to assume that every reader knows what they mean. According to *The Journey: A Bible for Seeking and Understanding Life* (Willow Creek Association, 1996; NIV), *mercy* is defined as "kindness and forgiveness, especially when given to a person who doesn't deserve it" (p. 1,686). Grace is described as "an undeserved favor or gift; the kindness and mercy that God gives us" (p. 1,680). Although the definitions of these two words sound very similar, there is a distinction. Grace allows us to receive favor and pardon but also enables us to endure anything that God allows in our lives, handling it to the best of our ability along with the guidance of the Holy Spirit. Mercy is a little different. By granting mercy, God is going easy on us, *not* giving us what we deserve due to the sins of our flesh but giving us pardon, being kind, and, in a way, letting us off the hook from getting what we truly deserve. As Peter wrote in 1 Peter 1:3 (NIV), "Praise be to the God and Father of our Lord Jesus Christ! In His great mercy, He has given us new birth into a living hope through the resurrection of Jesus Christ from the dead." God wanted to give us new life and cleanse us from our sinful nature, so He showed us mercy by sending His Son to the cross on our behalf. Jesus didn't come to judge but to save, as written in John 12:47 (NIV). God issues judgment when we pass from this life to the next, but on this earth, I am sure that God has pardoned all of us thousands of times by not giving us the outcomes that we truly deserve. I like to say that God withheld from giving us the kick in the booty that we needed but may not have gotten because He loves us so much. Sure, there is correction and there are consequences for our actions, and there will be a day when God will show us all that was waiting for us but that He spared us with His merciful heart. I know that my mouth has gotten me in trouble big time, and I have done things that were not very pleasing to God; but God has spared me plenty. Sometimes I can just sense the mercy of God falling down on me. Aren't we blessed that we have an amazingly loving Father?

The apostle Paul wrote in Romans 9:15–16 and verse 18 (NIV), "For he says to Moses, 'I will have mercy on whom I have mercy, and I will have compassion on whom I have compassion.' It does not, therefore, depend on man's desire or effort, but on God's mercy. Therefore God has mercy on whom he wants to have mercy, and he hardens whom he wants to harden." What the Lord is saying here is that it is His prerogative to decide to whom He wants to show mercy; it is not up to us to decide. Again, we have all been recipients of his mercy at one time or another in our lives, so we have no right to question when or to whom God is being merciful or how often He extends His merciful hand to any of us.

Throughout the Bible, there is talk about God being a just God, which He is. He is a righteous God who will avenge our enemies. Romans 12:19 (AMP) says, "Beloved, never avenge yourselves, but leave the way open for [God's] wrath; for it is written, Vengeance is Mine, I will repay (requite), says the Lord." God is faithful and will fight our battles for us. However, He is a gentle God, too, who has mercy. Of course, He wants to give us correction and bring conviction to His people through the prompting of the Holy Spirit when we do something that is contradictory to the Word of God. There are consequences to our actions, as Paul described in Galatians 6:7 (AMP): "Do not be deceived and deluded and misled; God will not allow Himself to be sneered at (scorned, disdained, or mocked by mere pretensions or professions, or by His precepts being set aside). [He inevitably deludes himself who attempts to delude God.] For whatever a man sows that and that only is what he will reap." However, God will also grant mercy because He loves us so much and wants us to learn from our mistakes. As I like to say when I declare my sins to the Lord and ask for pardon, "Lord, please go easy on me in terms of the consequences, for you know my heart and you know my flesh is mad weak!" In other words, have mercy on me, Father! In Micah 6:8 (NIV), it is written, "He has showed you, O man, what is good, and what does the Lord require of you? To act justly and to love mercy and to walk humbly with your God." God wants us to love mercy—to love kindness and gentleness and also demonstrate mercy to others on whom we may cast down judgment. Because the Lord goes easy on us so often, He asks that we do the same with others.

The second reason that this chapter is special to me is because it talks about Grace, the second "twin" who walks with Mercy. I truly experienced the fullness of God's grace almost two years ago when my mother unexpectedly died of a heart attack at age sixty-two. Before that day, I read and sometimes quoted 2 Corinthians 12:9 (NIV), which says, "My grace is sufficient for you, for my power is made perfect in your weakness." This is what the Lord spoke to Paul about the thorn that was stuck in his flesh, which Paul pleaded with God to take away from him. God did not remove the thorn but gave Paul the grace, or the ability (the "favor with Him"), to bear it. On the day of my mother's death, and every day thereafter, I got to experience that grace firsthand. I felt as if God had put me in a protective "grace bubble," as I was numb to many of my emotions when my mom first died and then for a few months afterward because, at first, we had a funeral to plan and people to inform of her death, and later we had paperwork to process and oh so many details of life to manage. I also moved in with my then ninety-three-year-old grandmother for a month until we could admit her into a nursing facility to live because she could no longer be left alone. (I work full-time and no other family member was available to care for her on a full-time basis.) I had to balance going to my apartment, coping with my hurt and adjustment to this major life change, and then going to Granny's place when home attendants were off duty. In some moments, I felt physically ill and my blood pressure was very high as a result of the grief, but His grace was sufficient. Whenever I felt His grace fall down on me, my blood pressure decreased and my anxiety level was put back in check. God gave me certain times each day when I would steal away to my apartment and cry, be ministered to by my circle of friends over the telephone, or listen to some praise and worship music in order to get back on track. Second Corinthians 12:9 came alive for me when my mom died. I find it so ironic that God would give life to a Scripture as a result of death. But that is how God works—He gives you the ability to cope. I would not be here today, writing this book, had it not been for the grace of God in handling that devastating situation, as well as many other hardships in life. God's hand of grace is so special that I don't even think that my description of how it kept me even does it justice! I know that we all have our own grace stories to share, and I pray that you all find a "grace place" that God can create for you to go and hide away as you wait for Him to fill up that "grace cup" so that you can keep drinking, which means to keep it moving, going through what God has you enduring in each tough season of life.

When we endure tragedy, hardships, difficult times, trials, and tribulations, His grace is sufficient. And when we are in sin, grace is there, too, to save the day. The more we sin, the more grace God will instill upon us. Now, that is not a license to commit sin; it is just good to know that there is a safety net that will catch us when we fall (the "grace net"). In Romans 5:20–21 (NIV), Paul wrote to the church, "The law was added so that the trespass might increase. But where sin increased, grace increased all the more, so that, just as sin reigned in death, so also grace might reign through righteousness to bring eternal life through Jesus Christ our Lord." We are saved by His grace (undeserved favor), and we are also justified by it, too. As Titus wrote (3:7 NIV), "So that, having been justified by His grace, we might become heirs having the hope of eternal life." Ephesians 2:4–5 (NIV) says, "But because of His great love for us, God, who is rich in mercy, made us alive with Christ even when we were dead in our transgressions—it is by grace you have been saved." We are entitled to walk with grace and mercy based on the gift of salvation, and they have our backs in every situation.

Mercy and Grace are the twins that God provided us when He purchased us with the blood of Jesus. I capitalized the *M* in "Mercy" and the *G* in "Grace" in certain places throughout the chapter as if they were actual names of people so that, if you are practical like me, it will be an easy reminder to help you call upon the Lord but also call "your girls" for reinforcements through each day. Here are some Scriptures to remember when you are in need of "The Twins," all taken from the Amplified Bible.

> Psalm 32:10—"Many are the sorrows of the wicked, but he who trusts in, relies on, and confidently leans on the Lord shall be compassed about with mercy and with loving-kindness."

> Psalm 84:11—"For the Lord God is a Sun and Shield; the Lord bestows [present] grace and favor and [future] glory (honor, splendor, and heavenly bliss)! No good thing will He withhold from those who walk uprightly."

> Psalm 94:18—"When I said, My foot is slipping, Your mercy and loving-kindness, O Lord, held me up."

> Psalm 103:10–11—"He has not dealt with us after our sins nor rewarded us according to our iniquities. For as the heavens are high above the earth, so great are His mercy and loving-kindness toward those who reverently and worshipfully fear Him."

> Psalm 118:1—"O give thanks to the Lord, for He is good; for His mercy and loving-kindness endure forever."

> Ephesians 2:4–5—"But God—so rich is He in His mercy! Because of and in order to satisfy the great and wonderful and intense love with which He loved us, even when we were dead

(slain) by [our own] shortcomings and trespasses, He made us alive together in fellowship and in union with Christ; [He gave us the very life of Christ Himself, the same new life with which He quickened Him, for] it is by grace (His favor and mercy which you did not deserve) that you are saved (delivered from judgment and made partakers of Christ's salvation)."

Hebrews 4:16—"Let us then fearlessly and confidently and boldly draw near to the throne of grace (the throne of God's unmerited favor to us sinners), that we may receive mercy [for our failures] and find grace to help in good time for every need [appropriate help and well-timed help, coming just when we need it]."

CHAPTER 7

Trust, Obey, and Forgive

The Lord spoke to me about a month ago when I was in a state of panic about a particular situation. I was thinking irrational thoughts that were keeping me from getting to sleep one night. I was in the bathroom where, oddly enough, God gives me a lot of revelations. The Holy Spirit spoke three words to me, not in an audible voice as I would hear a live person, but in my mind, heart, soul, and spirit. I heard, "Trust, obey, and forgive." Those were three areas in my life in which I was lacking and that had been blocking many of the blessings that the Lord had for me—for years. I have not been the same since that night. God wanted me to clean up my act in those areas (maybe that is why He gave me the revelation in the bathroom), and it has been challenging but necessary in order for me to get to the next level in my walk with Jesus and to receive what He has waiting for me. I must note that God is still refining me in these areas, and deliverance is on its way, in the name of Jesus!

"Lean on, trust in, and be confident in the Lord with all your heart and mind and do not rely on your own insight or understanding. In all your ways know, recognize, and acknowledge Him and He will direct and make straight and plain your paths" (Prov. 3:5–6 AMP). I have recited, memorized, and quoted this very popular Scripture for years now; it's one of my favorites. But, I must be honest—I had not been living it. You see, I come from a long line of worriers; from what I can recall from stories about my family, the worry gene goes back to my great-grandmother and was definitely passed down to my grandmother (who is fondly known as Granny), my mother (who is deceased), and now my siblings and me, and I even sense an element of it in my little niece. There has always been a spirit of anxiety in my family, sometimes along with spirits of doubt, fear, and dread (angst). It has been so extreme that some family members have even been diagnosed with anxiety disorders and have been prescribed anti-anxiety medication in order to cope on a daily basis. I am not rationalizing worry, nor am I making excuses for it; I am merely explaining the root of it in my bloodline as I prepare to share more on it as well as talk about how the Lord is dealing with me in this area of my life—trust.

The day that Dr. Bond prophesied about this book, she also had other messages from the Lord for me. One of the most disturbing truths that the Holy Spirit spoke through her was that I worry—and that I worry too much. The kicker was that she continued with, "And that is a sin." I was shocked to hear that I was sinning against God by worrying, much less by worrying too much. I thought I had my anxiety under control, especially because I am a Christian serving God. But you can be a Christian, serving God, reading your Word, being in prayer, and ministering to others—which I did on a regular basis, always in and out of the church building—but still be a worrier!

Granted, my family has always erred on the side of being pessimistic, thinking the worst. Ironically, that is the exact thing that I get on my Granny's case about, for she is the Queen Mother of "What if the worst thing happens?" I am just a mere princess! I joke with this because it is my nature to joke around, but I am not making light of the fact that this is a huge problem. I am using this analogy simply to illustrate the point that my Granny's anxiety extends to the utmost degree, but mine is not too far behind. My anxiety is camouflaged, while Granny has no filter on hers. God wants me to know that I am a princess but that I am *His* princess, because He is the King. However, He is not going to tolerate my being a princess of worry; His will is that I represent His kingdom as a princess of trust.

The revelation that I was more anxious than I perceived myself to be was a bitter pill to swallow; I knew I was anxious, but I didn't think that I was *that* anxious! Dr. Bond's message was the water with which I needed to swallow that pill, but it was also the cold water in the face that I needed to be splashed on me so I could get the worrying under control. I have to learn to master it—1 Peter 5:7 (AMP) encourages us to entrust our lives to God, "casting the whole of your care [all your anxieties, all your worries, all your concerns, once and for all] on Him, for He cares for you affectionately and cares about you watchfully."

After I came to the Lord, I had a handle on that "family jewel" that I inherited, that spirit of anxiety that has overshadowed us for generations. I used to joke and say that it was neurotic Italian family syndrome, but I now know that it is a spirit that wants to infiltrate my mind and take over my life. I believe that, after my mother died, I lost a bit of the handle that I had on my anxiety, and I allowed my mind to run wild a bit because of the grief that I had just experienced. Although many extended family members had died in the past, this was the first member of my immediate family to die, and it was my beloved mother. It was an unexpected death that occurred two days before Christmas. When something hits you that suddenly, it tends to make you more fearful of the unexpected. For months thereafter, a spirit of dread followed me like a black cloud, but I did not confess it to many people. I believe Satan was playing on my hurt and wanted me get caught up in worrying about all of the remaining family members, using this as a major distraction in my life. Intrusive thoughts would plague me at unexpected times of the day and night. I would have dreams about family members' getting hurt and would get up at various times of the night to intercede for them. We must always remember that fear is not from God: "For God did not give us a spirit of timidity (of cowardice, of craven and cringing and fawning fear), but [He has given us a spirit] of power and of love and of calm and well-balanced mind and discipline and self-control" (2 Tim. 1:7 AMP). So, whenever those thoughts come to my mind to haunt my spirit, I have to cast my care on the Lord, as Peter advised in his epistle (1 Peter 5:7 NIV).

God created us, and if we are His, He is really the only one on whom we can depend. Jesus cautioned us against worrying in Matthew 6:25–34 (AMP). It is one of the more popular Scriptures in the New Testament, and, again, I have memorized it and quoted it on several occasions; yet it is only in this season of my life that God has had to "pull on my coattails" about owning it and walking in the comfort that it brings.

> Therefore I tell you, stop being perpetually uneasy (anxious and worried) about your life, what you shall eat or what you

shall drink; or about your body, what you shall put on. Is not life greater [in quality] than food, and the body [far above and more excellent] than clothing? Look at the birds of the air; they neither sow nor reap nor gather into barns, and yet your heavenly Father keeps feeding them. Are you not worth much more than they? And who of you by worrying and being anxious can add one unit of measure (cubit) to his stature or to the span of his life? And why should you be anxious about clothes? Consider the lilies of the field and learn thoroughly how they grow; they neither toil nor spin. Yet I tell you, even Solomon in all his magnificence (excellence, dignity, and grace) was not arrayed like one of these. But if God so clothes the grass of the field, which today is alive and green and tomorrow is tossed into the furnace, will He not much more surely clothe you, O you of little faith? Therefore do not worry and be anxious, saying, what are we going to have to eat? Or, what are we going to have to drink? Or, what are we going to have to wear? For the Gentiles (heathen) wish for and crave and diligently seek all these things, and your heavenly Father knows well that you need them all. But seek (aim at and strive after) first of all His kingdom and His righteousness (His way of doing and being right), and then all these things taken together will be given you besides. So do not worry or be anxious about tomorrow, for tomorrow will have worries and anxieties of its own. Sufficient for each day is its own trouble.

Because this is a very meaty portion of Scripture, we need to digest it and really meditate on it. I am not going to dissect it like I did the Lord's Prayer, but I will summarize for you what God wants us to know by grabbing a hold of this in our hearts. God created the universe and everything in it, but He created man and woman with the main purpose of having a relationship with Him that no other creature can possibly have. God created humans to have souls (emotions, intellect, and reasoning); therefore, we are the only creations who can communicate, think, have a conscience, know right from wrong, and live for the Lord. So if God is going to take care of the birds and the flowers, making sure that they get their "daily bread," will He not ensure that we will have our provisions—for body, mind, soul, heart, and spirit? In verse 33, Jesus says that we have to seek the kingdom of God *first*, and *then* everything else will be given to us.

If we are anxious, worried, or thinking that we are without what we need, we have to look up to the hills, from whence cometh our help (Ps. 121:1 KJV). I have spent many years looking at mankind, which leaves me prone to comparisons and competitions—every reason to get out of God's will and into jealousy, envy, dissatisfaction, and strife. We cannot look within too much. It is good to be introspective in order to receive conviction and take responsibility for our actions. But if we keep the focus on ourselves constantly, then we become self-centered.

There were also times in my life when I would look behind me—dwelling on and sometimes obsessing about past mistakes, hurts, and challenges. What good does that do? The past is history. It is good to have memories and reflect on the good, but we must let go of the bad and the ugly that have happened. If we don't, we will be in a pit out of which it is very difficult to climb. And if we look ahead too much, we will miss the here and now, which is God's gift to us (the "present"). However, we need to press forward while looking upward for help. The apostle Paul wrote in Philippians 3:12–14 (AMP),

> Not that I have now attained [this ideal], or have already been made perfect, but I press on to lay hold of (grasp) and make my own, that for which Christ Jesus (the Messiah) has laid hold of me and made me His own. I do not consider, brethren, that I have captured and made it my own [yet]; but one thing I do [it is my one aspiration]: forgetting what lies behind and straining forward to what lies ahead, I press on toward the goal to win the [supreme and heavenly] prize to which God in Christ Jesus is calling us upward.

As Matthew 6:34 states, tomorrow is going to have its own set of worries, and God has not yet given us that daily bread. So we have to stay in the present, looking nowhere but up. As a result, that anxiety will lessen. That is how we can build our trust, knowing that our heavenly Father, with whom we have a relationship and who has not failed us, will take care of every issue.

The second word God spoke to me that night, *obey*, referred to my disobedience, which is also a "blessing blocker." For years, I had not been totally obedient to the Lord, and the Lord deals with me in this area on a regular basis. I would be convicted of a particular sin, confess it, walk away for a few weeks or month or so, and then find myself right back in the same mess again. When we sin, the Holy Spirit within us is grieved (saddened), and our fellowship with the Lord needs to be restored. The Lord is merciful, and when we confess our sins to Him, this restoration does come. However, if we keep confessing the same sins over and over again but do not repent or turn away from the behavior, then are we truly sorry that we have sinned against God?

For a number of years, I prayed for one particular thing. I had my prayer partners touching and agreeing in prayer with me so that God would bless me in that area of my life. One of my prayer partners, whom I fondly call my Mother in Christ, was in prayer and fasting about the issue over a period of years. Finally, the Holy Spirit spoke to her and gave her "many a word" for me in reference to my sin. Actually, the Holy Spirit directed her to stop enabling me and start giving "tough love" and a strong word about the issue. She had been sugarcoating the situation, being encouraging, merciful, and also sharing how she had struggled in a similar area in a season of her life many years earlier. Well, I needed to hear all of that. It brought me to a place where I realized that there comes a time when God wants us to take responsibility for and own up to our part in a matter and walk away from what we are doing. As John 14:15 (AMP) says, "If you [really] love Me, you will keep (obey) My commands."

My prayer partners and I had all been flooding heaven with prayers for blessing, but God can't bless what we are blocking. He will not bless disobedience in the life of a believer. At one point, I saw everyone else around me being blessed, and the Lord spoke to me and said (paraphrasing), "Do not concern yourself with the affairs of others because you answer for *you* and *you alone*. You will give an account for *your* life, and not for anyone else. And, because you are in a covenant relationship with me, *you know better than that* in terms of what pleases me and what doesn't." Ouch! *That was rough*, I thought. Then, I would run the whole "I am in ministry and I serve you, Lord, so why aren't you blessing me?" thing by the Lord, as if He couldn't see my true mind and heart. Yes, we can serve and minister—we can sacrifice, just as the Israelites did in the Old Testament, but are we being obedient? In 1 Samuel 15:22 (KJV), Samuel, the prophet, said, "Hath the LORD as great delight in burnt offerings and sacrifices, as in obeying the voice of the LORD? Behold, to obey is better than sacrifice, and to hearken than the fat of rams." In other words, even though the Israelites were sacrificing to the Lord, they were being disobedient by worshipping other gods. God wasn't going to bless them because their obedience toward Him was more important than the sacrifices that they made. So it is with us today. We can do everything godly in the eyes of man, but if we are not obeying what the Word tells us, we will not prosper in the areas in which we are sinning.

Sometimes we rationalize our sins, thinking that we can get by with certain behaviors, or we sometimes "test the waters" to see how much we can get away with. Regardless of what type of sin you are committing, someone is always going to get hurt and be affected in the long run. Even enjoying the things of the world can be considered disobedience, especially if the Lord is asking you to "lay something down," such as worldly entertainment or a lifestyle that is not in alignment with His will. As Christians, sometimes we tend to "dabble" in the things of the world, having one foot in the church and the other foot in the world. I did that for years. Also, when you justify sin or look at other people's lifestyles in comparison to your own and determine that your sin is "not as bad" as the next person's, that is a big problem. God grabbed a hold of me years ago regarding this, and now I always take a moment to take the speck out of my own eye, as instructed by Jesus in Matthew 7:3–5 (NIV): "Why do you stare from without at the very small particle that is in your brother's eye but do not become aware of and consider the beam of timber that is in your own eye? Or how can you say to your brother, Let me get the tiny particle out of your eye, when there is the beam of timber in your own eye? You hypocrite, first get the beam of timber out of your own eye, and then you will see clearly to take the tiny particle out of your brother's eye." I cannot speak a word into someone else's life about sin unless I deal with the sin in my own life first. We really need to seek the Lord in this area and ask God to show us *any* area of our lives that is displeasing to Him. From there, we need to ask for the grace to lay down whatever we need to surrender. He has so much more in store for us after we do this!

The bottom line is that it was I who was the holdup in my blessing—I couldn't blame God, man, generational curses, or the Devil. It was my own flesh that was in the way. I wanted the victory over the sin but was not willing to do my part. I wanted God to turn me off of any ungodly desires, yet God was telling me on His own and through my Mother in Christ and other prayer partners to turn *myself* off. The grace was there, but I chose to give in to the temptation. My behavior was not right, my thought process needed to be renewed, and I needed true repentance. Until I completely walked away with a right heart, I was going to stay stuck in that one area. Sure, I was prospering in almost every other area of my life, but this area was not going to grow until I fully surrendered. God is not going to bless disobedience, although on the outside, to the world, it may look like someone is getting away with a blessing despite his or her disobedience. God will withhold until we are ready, until we give up the junk, and then He can release the blessing that He so wants to give us.

Throughout the Bible, God used many people who trusted and obeyed Him even though they were probably scared out of their minds at times. For example, God called Abraham to be the father of the nations and promised him a son (read Gen. 17–22). That son, Isaac, came, and then years after Abraham had been promised, God tested him to see if he would sacrifice his son on the altar, giving him up to the Lord. Abraham put his son on the chopping block even though the Lord had promised Isaac to him and he had waited so long to have him. Abraham trusted and obeyed, and as a result of his obedience, God spared Isaac's life. Moses, in the Book of Exodus, was commanded by the Lord to lead the Israelites out of captivity by speaking to Pharaoh (chapter 9), although he had a lot of insecurities (namely, a stuttering problem), and Moses obeyed. In Joshua 6, Moses's protégé marched around Jericho seven times (seems silly, right?) because the Lord had commanded him to do so, and then the walls came tumbling down. Daniel and his three friends—Shadrach, Meshach, and Abednego—would not bow down to the idols in King Nebuchadnezzar's court (Daniel 1–3). Daniel's three friends were placed in a fiery furnace to burn and die; they came out without a burn on them but with a fourth person (the Lord!), even though the heat was unbearable. Later, Daniel was placed in a den to be eaten by lions, but the Lord closed the lions' mouths so Daniel would not lose his life. These young Hebrew boys did not compromise their faith, did not bow down to idols. Instead, they put their trust in the Lord, and because of their obedience, their lives were spared and the hearts of some of those around them—namely, the king—were changed, all for the glory of God.

We cannot forget my two favorite women in the Old Testament, Ruth and Esther. Ruth was loyal to her mother-in-law, Naomi, after Naomi's and Ruth's husbands, along with one of Naomi's sons, were killed in battle. Ruth decided to live with Naomi after their deaths instead of going back to her homeland. Because of the trust that she put in the God of Naomi's people (the Lord Jehovah), Ruth found favor with a relative of Naomi's deceased husband, Boaz, and later married him. Ruth ended up being in the bloodline of Jesus because of her trust in and obedience to what the Lord instructed her to do through Naomi's and Boaz's direction. Another Old Testament woman, Esther, was a young, orphaned Jewish girl who trusted the Lord—and waited on Him, too, for a year—to be made queen. She had to go before her king and request pardon for the Jewish people, for there was a plot to destroy the entire nation, which could have cost Esther her life even though she was the queen. Esther trusted and obeyed her Lord on behalf of her people. The stories of Ruth and Esther are found in books that bear their names, and they are very short and easy but meaningful reads that speak about loyalty, trust, and obedience.

In the New Testament, Mary and Joseph, Jesus' earthly parents, definitely had to trust and obey in a time when a woman's having a baby out of wedlock was not acceptable. Mary was not impregnated the usual way but via immaculate conception, but who was going to believe her when she said that this was from the Lord? Angels spoke to both of them about what was expected of them, and both Mary and Joseph agreed to do their part (Matthew 1:18–24). And let's not forget what the apostles had to endure, trusting Jesus, leaving their livelihoods, and becoming "fishers of men" (Matt. 4:19 NIV), as well as what they faced after Jesus' resurrection when they went to preach the good news to the entire world. In Luke 22:42 (NIV), Jesus even said during His last hours in the

Garden of Gethsemane, "Father, if you are willing, take this cup from me; yet not my will, but yours be done." He wanted to trust and obey, even if it meant His death—and it did.

David said in Psalm 96:1 (AMP), "O sing to the Lord a new song; sing to the Lord, all the earth!" David is emphasizing that it is important to sing that new song because it is tiring and self-defeating to sing the same ol' song of self-pity all the time. In my life, it is in the areas of trusting and obeying God, and also forgiving others and myself, that the old song is getting played out, although the Lord takes us just as we are and is very patient with our sanctification process. We have to think as well as feel differently about what is on our minds and hearts. If it is not in alignment with God's Word, we need to seek His Word daily in order to be in one accord with Him. In other words, we have to change our mind-sets if we are going to have any victory in our lives. As Paul wrote to the Romans in chapter 12, verse 2 (AMP), "Do not be conformed to this world (this age), [fashioned after and adapted to its external, superficial customs], but be transformed (changed) by the [entire] renewal of your mind [by its new ideals and its new attitude], so that you may prove [for yourselves] what is the good and acceptable and perfect will of God, even the thing which is good and acceptable and perfect [in His sight for you]." When we are troubled in our hearts, harboring sins in them, all we need to do is go to the Lord and ask for what David requested of the Lord in Psalm 51:10–12 (AMP): "Hide Your face from my sins and blot out all my guilt and iniquities. Create in me a clean heart, O God, and renew a right, persevering, and steadfast spirit within me. Cast me not away from Your presence and take not Your Holy Spirit from me. Restore to me the joy of Your salvation and uphold me with a willing spirit."

David was not right with God in a few areas of his life, even though he was a man after God's own heart (Acts 13:22 AMP). The apostle Paul wrote candidly in Romans 7:15–16 (AMP), "For I do not understand my own actions [I am baffled, bewildered]. I do not practice or accomplish what I wish, but I do the very thing that I loathe [which my moral instinct condemns]. Now if I do [habitually] what is contrary to my desire, [that means that] I acknowledge and agree that the Law is good (morally excellent) and that I take sides with it." Paul did the things that he did not want to do and ended up not doing what he needed to do at times, and he was the author of half of the New Testament! However, saying, "Great! David and Paul were disobedient, so I can disobey God, too," is not what I am suggesting. What I *am* saying is that we should feel a sense of relief that these two amazing men of God struggled just like we do and that what God did for them, He can do for us, too. Remember Romans 2:11 (AMP), "For God shows no partiality (undue favor or unfairness; with Him one man is not different from another)."

The third word is *forgiveness*, letting people off the hook by releasing them from your emotions of rejection, hurt, bitterness, anger, and so on. I am not going to spend much time on this subject because we covered it in Chapter 4, but I do provide Scriptures at the end of this chapter for your meditation. As we read in Chapter 4, "we must forgive those who trespass against us," as much as it hurts us to do so. Sometimes we think that the more we harbor unforgiveness, the more we hurt the party who has injured us. Well, that thinking is all wrong. The more we harbor those feelings, the more we hurt ourselves and drown in a sea of resentment. We saw in Matthew 18:35 that if we do not forgive others, God will not forgive us. That is a serious blessing blocker as well as a factor in our psychological and physical conditions. Many people suffer from anxiety, depression, high blood pressure, diabetes (high levels of sugar), intestinal issues, and so on because they hold onto hurts, which are buried deeply in their hearts and manifesting physically to harm the body, mind, and soul. The Lord spoke to me about forgiveness, and I came to the conclusion that I will have to ask Him to forgive me daily. I will also need to ask Him to help me forgive those who have hurt me, even if I have brought this request to Him thousands of times before. I have to surrender daily. That is the only way that I am going to be able to move forward, and God will hear me every time.

The following is a list of Scriptures on trust, obedience, and forgiveness on which you can meditate. Some of these verses have already been featured within the text of this chapter, and others will complement what you have already read. All Scriptures were taken from the Amplified Bible.

Trust

Psalm 27:1—"The Lord is my Light and my Salvation—whom shall I fear or dread? The Lord is the Refuge and Stronghold of my life—of whom shall I be afraid?"

Isaiah 26:3—"You will guard him and keep him in perfect and constant peace whose mind [both its inclination and its character] is stayed on You, because he commits himself to You, leans on You, and hopes confidently in You."

Isaiah 41:10—"Fear not [there is nothing to fear], for I am with you; do not look around you in terror and be dismayed, for I am your God. I will strengthen and harden you to difficulties, yes, I will help you; yes, I will hold you up and retain you with My [victorious] right hand of rightness and justice."

John 14: 27—"Peace I leave with you; My [own] peace I now give and bequeath to you. Not as the world gives do I give to you. Do not let your hearts be troubled, neither let them be afraid. [Stop allowing yourselves to be agitated and disturbed; and do not permit yourselves to be fearful and intimidated and cowardly and unsettled.]"

Obey

Deuteronomy 11:26–28—"Behold, I set before you this day a blessing and a curse—the blessing if you obey the commandments of the Lord your God which I command you this day; and the curse if you will not obey the commandments of the Lord your God, but turn aside from the way which I command you this day to go after other gods, which you have not known."

1 Kings 2:3–4—"Keep the charge of the Lord your God, walk in His ways, keep His statutes, His commandments, His precepts, and His testimonies, as it is written in the Law of Moses, that you may do wisely and prosper in all that you do and wherever you turn, that the Lord may fulfill His promise to me, saying,

If your sons take heed to their way, to walk before Me in truth with all their heart and mind and with all their soul, there shall not fail you [to have] a man on the throne of Israel."

Jeremiah 27:3—"But this thing I did command them: Listen to and obey My voice, and I will be your God and you will be My people; and walk in the whole way that I command you, that it may be well with you."

Matthew 6:21–24—"For where your treasure is, there will your heart be also. The eye is the lamp of the body. So if your eye is sound, your entire body will be full of light. But if your eye is unsound, your whole body will be full of darkness. If then the very light in you [your conscience] is darkened, how dense is that darkness! No one can serve two masters; for either he will hate the one and love the other, or he will stand by and be devoted to the one and despise and be against the other. You cannot serve God and mammon (deceitful riches, money, possessions, or whatever is trusted in)."

Hebrews 12:11—"For the time being no discipline brings joy, but seems grievous and painful; but afterwards it yields a peaceable fruit of righteousness to those who have been trained by it [a harvest of fruit which consists in righteousness—in conformity to God's will in purpose, thought, and action, resulting in right living and right standing with God]."

Forgive

Psalm 32:1–2—"Blessed (happy, fortunate, to be envied) is he who has forgiveness of his transgression continually exercised upon him, whose sin is covered. Blessed (happy, fortunate, to be envied) is the man to whom the Lord imputes no iniquity and in whose spirit there is no deceit."

Matthew 6:14–15—"For if you forgive people their trespasses [their reckless and willful sins, leaving them, letting them go, and giving up resentment], your heavenly Father will also forgive you. But if you do not forgive others their trespasses [their reckless and willful sins, leaving them, letting them go, and giving up resentment], neither will your Father forgive you your trespasses."

Ephesians 4:26–27, 31–32—"When angry, do not sin; do not ever let your wrath (your exasperation, your fury or indignation) last until the sun goes down. Leave no [such] room or foothold for the devil [give no opportunity to him]. Let all bitterness and indignation and wrath (passion, rage, bad temper) and resentment (anger, animosity) and quarreling (brawling, clamor, contention) and slander (evil-speaking, abusive or blasphemous language) be banished from you, with all malice (spite, ill will, or baseness of any kind). And become useful and helpful and kind to one another, tenderhearted (compassionate, understanding, loving-hearted), forgiving one another [readily and freely], as God in Christ forgave you."

In what areas of your life are you struggling? Where are you blocking your blessings? Where is there no fruit or growth in your life? I pray that you will take what I have shared, meditate on the Scriptures and the words of encouragement, and take all of your cares to the Lord so that He can give you instructions on how to move forward, releasing all that weighs you down and binds you. I pray freedom and victory for you, in the name of Jesus. As we go into the next chapter, remember that God will work this out for your good.

CHAPTER 8

He Can Work It Out

A song by the Beatles came out in 1965 entitled "We Can Work It Out." In God's economy, nothing can be further from the truth. We really can't work it out! The difference between the world and Christians is that we, as Christians, need to surrender our plans to the Lord so He can work it out and do it for our good. We have no power apart from the Holy Spirit. Sure, things come together for those who are not in Christ, but if we want God's best and live according to His will, we have to change the lyrics to this famous song and declare, "He Can Work It Out."

Romans 8:28 (AMP) is another popular Scripture in the Bible that states "We are assured and know that [God being a partner in their labor] all things work together and are [fitting into a plan] for good to and for those who love God and are called according to [His] design and purpose." Many people misquote this verse and simply say, "All things works together for good," leaving off "for those who love the Lord *and* are called according to His design and purpose." If you have no connection to Jesus, if you have not made Him your Lord and Savior, and if you are living out of the will of God for your life, then this Scripture doesn't apply to you. Only believers in Christ will benefit from this promise.

God works out every detail of our lives together for our good. Even when we don't think that the Lord is working, He is on the scene (behind the scenes, in front of the scenes, on top of the scenes—you get the picture) making sure that everything is in order and that every action and activity will flow together. For example, on the Wednesday morning my mother died, she was at home in her apartment with my father and brother. Ordinarily on Wednesday mornings, my mother would have been caring for my then two-year-old niece in the apartment, tending to her and preparing her breakfast. The regular Wednesday routine was that my sister (my niece's mom) would stay with my grandmother at her apartment nearby. My mom and sister often swapped caretaking responsibilities a few days a week so that my mom could enjoy my niece's company and my sister could tend to our then ninety-three-year-old grandmother's needs and have some downtime away from the baby. Because my niece had a virus, however, my sister and niece were at home in Brooklyn that day, and my mom, not feeling well herself, stayed in her own apartment, changing the schedule up a bit. And I was home on vacation because it was Christmas week. My mom had asked if I could stay with my grandmother so she could rest up and get to feeling better before Christmas. I truly believe that God worked it out so that my niece and sister would not be around and that I could be with my grandmother when my mother was dying. The irony of the whole situation was that my brother, who underestimates his ability to handle major life issues, was the one who was up with my mom, calling 9-1-1, and walking the operator through everything that was happening that morning. My father was awake for only a short period of time and already in shock over the possibility of my mom's dying, so I am not sure how effective Papa Cruz would have been in giving the paramedics what they needed to try to revive her. My brother stepped in and handled it as best as he could, with God's grace. God used my brother as the one to serve my mom in her last hour on earth, which I believe was something he needed to do, as she had always been the one to help him with his needs. I also believe that, out of us siblings, my brother was the one who could handle seeing my mom die. God knew that my sister and I could not. My brother has a calling on his life to serve and encourage others, so prayerfully God will use this to ignite his spirit into being all that God has created him to be!

God knew exactly where everyone was going to be the morning of my mother's death. In fact, He most likely knew how that day would shake out even before we were all born! Although the outcome was devastating and was not what any of us wanted, God caused all things to work together for our good—my vacation time, my niece's virus, my mom's illness, and so on so that the family members were exactly where they needed to be when the time came. In addition, my cousin had called me two days before with potentially bad news about his wife's health. The reason for the call was that he wanted me to pray for a good outcome. I prayed, but my prayers were not just about his wife; they were about my mom and our entire family—extended family as well—and I wasn't sure why, but the prayers were very intense. I felt the Holy Spirit descend on us over the phone to prepare us for what we did not know was ahead. My cousin reminded me about this prayer when I told him that my mom, who had been a second mother to him, had died. He said that God was preparing us for what was going to happen two days later. I believe that is why we were all in a state of numbness, more like a "grace bubble," and that was God's working every detail out for us.

Even through my mother's death, we all had to get to a higher level in our prayer lives and were given a higher level of grace, as well as the ability to fend for ourselves. My mom was a giver, a servant, a doer, and, many times, an enabler. She was an enabler because she didn't know how to balance out the gifts that God had given her; she was a pleaser who found it hard to say no to people, especially people whom she loved. Despite all of that, she lived what I called the "Romans 8:28 way." She had lost many loved ones along her journey—her grandfather and father when she was twenty; her older sister, who left behind two little boys, my cousins, then ages six and three, when she was twenty-two; her brother almost twenty years later; and her best friend, who was like her sister, five years later. She also experienced many other hardships in the family throughout the years. I never saw my mother bitter or angry with God about what she had lost. In fact, when I lived at home, I saw her at the kitchen table every morning, reading her prayer book. In our later years, I would ask my mom to reach out to friends who had lost their loved ones, and she did willingly. She had a heart for those who were mourning and those who were in need. God gave my mom the grace to share her heart with those who were experiencing things she had gone through. God turned Mama Cruz's sadness into a ministry. I used to say that my mom and I did ministry together—I did the praying, and she did the encouraging for those who were grieving. It was a privilege and an honor to "tag team" with her in ministry, even if it wasn't the conventional ministry service offered within the four walls of the church. It lasted only a few years, but I cherish that short season in our lives together.

God used another situation, which really frustrated all of us for about five years, to bring us closer together. My grandmother was getting sick, and it was no longer wise to leave her alone in her apartment at night. My mother offered the solution of my sister and me taking turns sleeping on my grandmother's sofa bed every night. Well, that irritated me because she didn't ask us; she *told* us what we were going to do. I was resentful for a long time, yet I could not disrespect my mother and grandmother and refuse them by saying, "No way!" If the shoe had been on the other foot, both women would have camped out on my couch to help me. Although there were many challenging moments during that season, the beautiful thing that God worked out for our good was that He allowed me to spend time with my mom in those last years before she died. She lived across the street from my grandmother, so I would go and have dinner with the family on some of the nights that I was "on duty" and enjoy quality time with them before going to Granny's place. Had my grandmother not been in need, I would not have been with my family as much and would have missed out on many nights with my beloved mother. I consider that wonderful yet sometimes trying time as a "Romans 8:28 season."

God doesn't use only devastating situations such as death to work things out for our good. He also uses day-to-day disappointments, turning rain into sunshine. I have gone through a lot of disappointment in the area of dating. There was one scenario in particular that was tough for me, especially because everyone liked the guy I was dating. I knew deep down in my spirit that the relationship would not work out, yet I went along for a ride. He was not the man God had for me. He was saved but had backslidden in terms of living for God. I was too early in my walk to understand the difference and thought that everything was good because he had a Christian faith. Let me explain the distinction. A saved person has received Christ and wants to, and does, make God first in his or her life. A backslidden person is saved but has "slidden backward" or fallen away from God and has turned to his or her old way of living (Prov. 14:14). Hosea 14:1–2 (AMP) says, "O Israel, return to the Lord your God, for you have stumbled and fallen, [visited by calamity] due to your iniquity. Take with you words and return to the Lord. Say to Him, Take away all our iniquity; accept what is good and receive us graciously; so will we render [our thanks] as bullocks [to be sacrificed] and pay the confession of our lips." And Jeremiah 3:14 (KJV) says, "'Return, O backsliding children,' says the Lord; 'for I am married to you. I will take you, one from a city and two from a family, and I will bring you to Zion.'" God is calling all backslidden Christians back to a heart of worship, especially anyone who is reading these three Scriptures right now! If you have gone down your own path, please come back to the one that God has for you; He will welcome you back with open arms.

Now, let's get back to the story. I just needed to add that side note as God put it on my heart. God was pulling me into a closer relationship with Him, so dating someone who truly didn't share the same heart for God probably would not have produced good fruit in my life. God needed to move that man off my path, for he was a distraction from what God wanted me to accomplish. I surely didn't know that way back then, but I certainly know it now. It was a period of my life when I had to learn that I couldn't compromise my values for anyone. This man was a sweetheart, but he was not a godly influence. Deep down, his heart was in the right place (he knew Jesus had saved him), but he struggled with alcoholism and fornication and had a rebellious spirit toward authority. That was a bad combination for my then controlling and sensual spirit. He was a "follower of man," not of God, which was clear to me even though he came from a godly home. In addition, he was hinting at moving into my apartment without being married to me, and that is a no-no in my book. To this day, I don't know if he ever came back to the Lord and God's way of living for him. I wish him well and have prayed for him since our breakup. The blessing that came out of this situation was that God put the brakes on that relationship because he wanted better for His daughter. For a long time, I had hard feelings, but now I am so grateful that God put an end to our relationship. God had taken this situation, as well as many others that led to breakups, so that I could have breakthroughs and clear my heart for exactly what and who He has in store for me. I thank the Lord for working all of that out for my good because he loves me and because I am trying my best to live according to His plan, purpose, and will for my life.

It is hard to grasp that all things will work together for our good, even evil. But as Joseph declared in Genesis 50:20 (NIV), "You intended to harm me, but God intended it for good to accomplish what is now being done, the saving of many lives." Joseph went through so much (Genesis 37–50) because his brothers were jealous of the favor that he had with their father and also of his ability to interpret dreams. They sold him into slavery and led Jacob, their father, to think that he had been killed by a wild animal. Joseph ended up being a right-hand man to Potiphar—chief officer to Pharaoh and ruler of Egypt—and living in a mansion. Joseph had favor there until Potiphar's wife started making advances toward him. When he didn't succumb to her temptations, she falsely accused him of rape, and Joseph was put in jail. Despite being in jail, Joseph had favor there, too, because of his ability to interpret dreams, which led him to another right-hand-man situation when he was released, only this time to Pharaoh! The irony of Joseph's story was that when famine struck the land years later, his brothers went to him (not knowing that it was he because they didn't expect him to be hanging with Pharaoh). They *needed* him so they could survive. Wow! The very same brothers who had sold him and left him for dead were the ones who needed a serious favor from him later in their lives when they were in a life-or-death situation themselves.

What Joseph was basically saying was that whatever the Enemy means for evil, God will work out for good. That means that God, who allows the Enemy to do what he does, giving us what God knows we can handle, will take every hurt and turn it into healing. When we turn our devastation to the Lord, He gives us beauty in exchange for the ashes (Isa. 61:3 NIV). For example, many pastors and preachers who speak internationally—some are the famous "televangelists" that we all know and love—as well as brothers and sisters in the faith who are not in the public eye, have powerful testimonies of drug abuse, alcoholism, molestation, sexual abuse, domestic violence, and so on. God has taken every bit of their misery and transformed it into ministry for them. Even my mother's many losses turned out to be a vehicle for her to minister from. God has taken their most trying seasons and allowed them to heal so that they can help others heal in those same areas. During the years of pain, these individuals had been given God's grace to endure the suffering associated with the trials. Because of healing, God "restores the years that the locusts have eaten" (Joel 2:2 NIV), bringing blessings, giving them the opportunity to share their hearts with the masses, making Genesis 50:20 and Romans 8:28 come alive for so many, and bringing more people to the Lord. We are going to talk more about restoration in a later chapter.

God allows us to go through hard times all for His glory. As written in John 16: 33 (AMP), "I have told you these things, so that in Me you may have [perfect] peace and confidence. In the world you have tribulation and trials and distress and frustration; but be of good cheer [take courage; be confident, certain, undaunted] for I have overcome the world. [I have deprived it of power to harm you and have conquered it for you.]" God will allow what He believes will be beneficial to us and also what He will give us the grace to handle, like Job in the Old Testament (who we will discuss in Chapter 15). So when you feel defeated (and, to be completely transparent, I am going through a season where I feel like throwing in the towel right now), just remember that Beatles song and change the chorus to "He can work it out." And He will.

CHAPTER 9

He's Got Our Backs!

I titled this chapter the way I did because I wanted to focus on God, our protector who covers us in "full armor" in battle. Yes, we are in a battle—a spiritual battle—but remember that the battle belongs to the Lord (Prov. 21:31). However, we are not battling against humans in the natural realm (on earth) but against the principalities of darkness. A principality is simply a territory ruled by a prince, so, principalities are any areas where darkness prevails. Satan is a prince of darkness, and he doesn't roam alone; he takes his little band of demons with him. Always remember, though, that our Savior, Jesus, is the Prince of Peace and prevails over the darkness. Hallelujah for that!

In Ephesians 6:10–18, Paul explains to the church in Ephesus that they need to put on their spiritual armor just as they put on their natural clothing every day. Spiritual clothing is just as important as natural clothing; we need both coverings because "our enemy the devil prowls around like a roaring lion looking for someone to devour" (1 Peter 5:8 NIV). Satan is not happy unless he is tripping us up, keeping us distracted and frustrated so we turn away from the will of God. Believers are a threat to the kingdom of darkness because we are the "light of the world" (Matt. 5:14 NIV) and light exposes the darkness. Therefore, the Enemy would love nothing more than for you to be killed, have things stolen from you, and be destroyed (John 10:10 NIV). In this chapter, we will take the verses of this passage of Scripture and discuss what body parts are being covered by the armor, why each part needs to be covered, and what to do to fight the Enemy daily. Let's go through the entire passage first and then break it down.

Finally, be strong in the Lord and in his mighty power. Put on the full armor of God, so that you can take your stand against the devil's schemes. For our struggle is not against flesh and blood, but against the rulers, against the authorities, against the powers of this dark world and against the spiritual forces of evil in the heavenly realms. Therefore put on the full armor of God, so that when the day of evil comes, you may be able to stand your ground, and after you have done everything, to stand. Stand firm then, with the belt of truth buckled around your waist, with the breastplate of righteousness in place, and with your feet fitted with the readiness that comes from the gospel of peace. In addition to all this, take up the shield of faith, with which you can extinguish all the flaming arrows of the evil one. Take the helmet of salvation and the sword of the Spirit, which is the word of God. (Eph. 6:10–18 NIV)

The first few lines tell us to be strong in God, which means to walk in our authority. As a believer, you have the Holy Spirit living inside you. God has dominion over your life, and you are covered by the blood of Jesus. Jesus bought your salvation with his blood, so Satan, or any of his crew of demons, does not have a hold on you. Your part in this battle is simply that you have to put on the armor and use it! The next verses go on to say what I stated in the beginning—you are not fighting the man or woman who is giving you a hard time but the spirits (or powers or dark forces) that operate in the spirit realm and that operate *through* that man or woman or several people at the same time. There is such a battle going on in the spirit realm that it manifests itself in the natural realm (earth), especially in this day because we are in End Times (read Matt. 24:3–13 to understand all of the signs of the end of the age). We have to know that man is not our enemy, but it is the Devil who tries to run people, wreaking havoc, sometimes even operating through believers if they are not guarded and if they open themselves to be used by the Devil and act up in their flesh, which pleases the Devil. It is even worse when there is a crack in the foundation of a believer and Satan can get a foothold into your world, where principalities can seep in and cause strife. On the day when evil strikes, you can stand firm and not be shaken, and you can prevent the Enemy from entering if your armor is on.

"Stand firm then, with the belt of truth buckled around your waist" is the next line; the belt (or girdle, as it is termed in other translations of the Bible) is the piece of armor that Paul instructs the saints in Ephesus to put on first. The waist is at the center, or core, of the body. In the natural realm, a belt is a supportive accessory that holds our pants in place. In a spiritual battle, we need a belt to wrap the truth around us so that our core is protected. A belt or girdle of truth is the Word of God. We need to fasten our belts in being secure about what God promises in the Word. My grandmother used to wear a girdle, and that thing was tight! It minimized the appearance of fat, which is why some women wear them, and it was so tight that nothing could get in. It looked like Granny couldn't breathe when she was wearing it. So our spiritual girdles serve to support us with truth so that no lies can enter our core to destroy our walk with God. Typically, the belts of Roman soldiers in the New Testament days were thick and covered their waists, like an apron, as well as the groin area to keep that section from being exposed to attack. In the spiritual battle, we want to make sure that our belts are on to prevent any attacks that may cause us to stray into sexual sin as defined in the Word, such as adultery, fornication, orgies, incest, rape, and so on. (Refer to Col. 3:5 AMP). And, in our day and age, we really need to keep ourselves protected from the temptations that are running rampant all around us, especially regarding sex.

"The breastplate of righteousness" is the next piece of armor, and it guards our hearts (our emotions). We need to know that we are the righteousness of God, so we need to keep that close to our hearts. Our hearts are our lifelines, and in an earthly battle, it is crucial that a soldier wear a breastplate, like a modern-day police officer wearing a bulletproof vest. In a spiritual battle, our hearts need protection as well because we can become very vulnerable, and when Satan attacks our hearts, or emotions, it affects our minds and our bodies.

"Feet fitted with the readiness that comes from the gospel of peace" are the next body parts to be covered with spiritual clothing. We need to walk in peace, knowing the Gospel. Basically, every piece of armor points to the Word. We have to walk in the Word of God, and we need to make sure that our feet are covered so that we don't walk—or, in some cases, run—into chaos, destruction, or sin. It's easy to walk in anxiety and depression with all that goes on around us today, but we have to maintain the peace that surpasses all understanding (Phil. 4:7 NIV). I like to put on my "gospel boots of peace." The Roman soldiers wore sandals, but I want to wear my warrior boots, even though earthly boots make my feet sweat. But they cover the feet completely, and I don't want any part of my "spiritual feet" exposed, not even a pinky toe. Forgive me for using a secular example, but I like to take worldly songs and use them in ministry in order to make the Word more applicable so that people can better understand it. Nancy Sinatra (daughter of Frank Sinatra) recorded a song in 1966 (before my time, folks!). It's called "These Boots Are Made for Walking," and the chorus goes, "These boots are made for walking, and that's just what they'll do. And one of these days these boots are gonna walk all over you." I know it's not a very nice thing to say to someone, but let's say it to the Devil. Let's walk all over him before he tries to walk all over us.

"In addition to all this, take up the shield of faith, with which you can extinguish all the flaming arrows of the evil one." What would a battle be without offense as well as defense? We definitely need to be shielded from attack; those arrows are indeed flaming. Satan brings fire—after all, he is from hell, and it is mighty hot down there. So whatever he throws at us is going to be burning hot! Our shields (our defense) are our faith—our belief that God will defend us, provide for us, protect us, and fight this battle for us even though he instructs us to put on our battle gear to be protected from Satan's attacks. Our shield of faith is carried in one hand and our sword of the spirit in the other hand. Our faith and the Holy Spirit go together. We will talk about the sword in a minute.

"Take the helmet of salvation" is the next line—of course, our heads need to be covered with a helmet. When we ride bicycles, motorcycles, and even scooters, it is important to wear a helmet. Because we are going on a spiritual ride every single day in battle, we need to put the protective gear on our heads. Physically, we need to protect our heads, which are at the top of our bodies, but we also need to protect our minds or thoughts. Satan knows what triggers negative, evil, carnal thoughts, those that are ultimately destructive. So that helmet has to prevent those types of thoughts from penetrating our minds each day. Again, by knowing the

Word of God, we can renew our minds and change our thinking, filling our minds with what God says about us and about what He wants for our lives. Just as the breastplate of righteousness guards our hearts, the helmet of salvation guards our minds. We are righteous because of our salvation, because of Jesus, not because we are the best soldiers on the battlefield. So we have to wear this gear with pride (not "puffed up" arrogance but pride in who we are in Christ).

"And the sword of the Spirit, which is the Word of God" is the last line; the sword is our weapon of offense. I can't emphasize enough that the Word of God is the most powerful weapon that a believer has with which to fight. A sword is the weapon that we use to "slice up" the principalities (sorry for sounding so aggressive!). Jesus carried His "sword" when He was fasting in the desert; any time the Devil came and tried to tempt Him, Jesus came back each time with the greatest weapon as a response: "It is written." He quoted the Father every time. Satan couldn't stand it and fled. However, in Luke 4:13 (AMP), it is written, "And when the devil had ended every [the complete cycle of] temptation, he [temporarily] left Him [that is, stood off from Him] until another more opportune and favorable time." So, know that even though Satan is defeated, he always comes back to fight when he sees an opportunity—an open door through which he sees where we are weak, vulnerable, distracted, frustrated, depressed, feeling low in spirit, and so on. If the Devil came back to tempt Jesus, you'd better believe that he will come back to tempt you, too. That is why we must be ready, wearing our armor, and sealing up every crack in the foundation so that the Enemy can't penetrate it.

In addition to putting on the full armor of God to stand against the principalities that want to come at us, we also need to stand on certain Scriptures to know that God has our backs. The Psalms are a great source of comfort when you need the Lord to defend you, so I am listing some Psalms below, along with a few other key Scriptures, for you to carry in battle. All Scriptures below are taken from the Amplified Bible.

> Psalm 3:1–4—"Lord, how they are increased who trouble me! Many are they who rise up against me. Many are saying of me, There is no help for him in God. Selah [pause, and calmly think

of that]! But You, O Lord, are a shield for me, my glory, and the lifter of my head. With my voice I cry to the Lord, and He hears and answers me out of His holy hill. Selah [pause, and calmly think of that]!"

Psalm 18:2–3—"The Lord is my Rock, my Fortress, and my Deliverer; my God, my keen and firm Strength in Whom I will trust and take refuge, my Shield, and the Horn of my salvation, my High Tower. I will call upon the Lord, Who is to be praised; so shall I be saved from my enemies."

Psalm 32:7—"You are a hiding place for me; You, Lord, preserve me from trouble, You surround me with songs and shouts of deliverance. Selah [pause, and calmly think of that]!"

Psalm 34:17–19—"When the righteous cry for help, the Lord hears, and delivers them out of all their distress and troubles. The Lord is close to those who are of a broken heart and saves such as are crushed with sorrow for sin and are humbly and thoroughly penitent. Many evils confront the [consistently] righteous, but the Lord delivers him out of them all."

Psalm 91—"He who dwells in the secret place of the Most High shall remain stable and fixed under the shadow of the Almighty [Whose power no foe can withstand]. I will say of the Lord, He is my Refuge and my Fortress, my God; on Him I lean and rely, and in Him I [confidently] trust! For [then] He will deliver you from the snare of the fowler and from the deadly pestilence. [Then] He will cover you with His pinions, and under His wings shall you trust and find refuge; His truth and His faithfulness are a shield and a buckler. You shall not be afraid of the terror of the night, nor of the arrow (the evil plots and slanders of the wicked) that flies by day, nor of the pestilence that stalks in darkness, nor of the destruction and sudden death that surprise and lay waste at noonday. A thousand may fall at your side, and ten thousand at your right hand, but it shall not come near you. Only a spectator shall you be [yourself inaccessible in the secret place of the Most High] as you witness the reward of the wicked.

Because you have made the Lord your refuge, and the Most High your dwelling place, there shall no evil befall you, nor any plague or calamity come near your tent. For He will give His angels [especial] charge over you to accompany and defend and preserve you in all your ways [of obedience and service]. They shall bear you up on their hands, lest you dash your foot against a stone. You shall tread upon the lion and adder; the young lion and the serpent shall you trample underfoot. Because he has set his love upon Me, therefore will I deliver him; I will set him on high, because he knows and understands My name [has a personal knowledge of My mercy, love, and kindness—trusts and relies on Me, knowing I will never forsake him, no, never]. He shall call upon Me, and I will answer him; I will be with him in trouble, I will deliver him and honor him. With long life will I satisfy him and show him My salvation."

Psalm 140—"Deliver me, O Lord, from evil men; preserve me from violent men; they devise mischiefs in their heart; continually they gather together and stir up wars. They sharpen their tongues like a serpent's; adders' poison is under their lips. Selah [pause, and calmly think of that]! Keep me, O Lord, from the hands of the wicked; preserve me from the violent men who have purposed to thrust aside my steps. The proud have hidden a snare for me; they have spread cords as a net by the wayside, they have set traps for me. Selah [pause, and calmly think of that]! I said to the Lord, You are my God; give ear to the voice of my supplications, O Lord. O God the Lord, the Strength of my salvation, You have covered my head in the day of battle. Grant not, O Lord, the desires of the wicked; further not their wicked plot and device, lest they exalt themselves. Selah [pause, and calmly think of that]! Those who are fencing me in raise their heads; may the mischief of their own lips and the very things they desire for me come upon them. Let burning coals fall upon them; let them be cast into the fire, into floods of water or deep water pits, from which they shall not rise. Let not a man of slanderous tongue be established in the earth; let evil hunt the violent man to overthrow him [let calamity follow his evildoings]. I know and rest in confidence upon it that the Lord will maintain the cause of the afflicted, and will secure justice for the poor and needy [of His believing children]. Surely the [uncompromisingly] righteous shall give thanks to Your name; the upright shall dwell in Your presence (before Your very face)."

In addition, hold onto the following two Scriptures that will sustain you, even if you feel like you are being taken down in the battle. Second Corinthians 4:8–9 (AMP) reads, "We are hedged in (pressed) on every side [troubled and oppressed in every way], but not cramped or crushed; we suffer embarrassments and are perplexed and unable to find a way out, but not driven to despair; we are pursued (persecuted and hard driven), but not deserted [to stand alone]; we are struck down to the ground, but never struck out and destroyed." And Isaiah 54:17 (AMP) declares, "But no weapon that is formed against you shall prosper, and every tongue that shall rise against you in judgment you shall show to be in the wrong. This [peace, righteousness, security, triumph over opposition] is the heritage of the servants of the Lord [those in whom the ideal Servant of the Lord is reproduced]; this is the righteousness or the vindication which they obtain from Me [this is that which I impart to them as their justification], says the Lord."

If you have learned nothing else by reading this chapter, grasp that the Word is the strongest weapon of all weapons we carry—the truth of Jesus Christ, His righteousness on us, our salvation, our faith, our peace, the Holy Spirit. As Hebrews 4:12 (AMP) indicates, "For the Word that God speaks is alive and full of power [making it active, operative, energizing, and effective]; it is sharper than any two-edged sword, penetrating to the dividing line of the breath of life (soul) and [the immortal] spirit, and of joints and marrow [of the deepest parts of our nature], exposing and sifting and analyzing and judging the very thoughts and purposes of the heart."

On a final note, I want to share one observation—there is no battle gear for the back. That is because we are fighting our enemy going forward, not retreating. And besides that, God has our backs, so we don't have to worry. Just put on your battle gear and invite the Lord in to be your bodyguard in this battle; your life belongs to Him anyway.

CHAPTER 10

Iron Sharpens Iron

In Chapter 9, I talked about protection from the Enemy's schemes in the form of spiritual battle gear. What I want to talk about now is another important aspect of our Christian walk—determining with whom we are walking. As a believer, it is critical to walk with other believers, as the Word of God commands us not to walk with those whose are not of Christ. As 2 Corinthians 6:14 (AMP) states, "Do not be unequally yoked with unbelievers [do not make mis-mated alliances with them or come under a different yoke with them, inconsistent with your faith]. For what partnership have right living and right standing with God with iniquity and lawlessness? Or how can light have fellowship with darkness?" *Yoked* is another way of saying "connected" or "intertwined," and this Scripture relates not only to whom we choose as our marriage partners but also to the circle of friends with whom we travel. It is important to remember that Jesus loved all people—saved and unsaved—because He and the Father are one and God *is* love. However, we must not get caught up in the day-to-day affairs of those who are not like-minded (Christ-minded). But know that God can put people to whom He wants us to minister and ultimately receive Christ in our paths. God has to speak to you directly about who those individuals are. I am grateful for the saints who befriended me, invited me into their homes, loved me, answered my questions, and planted seeds along my journey—despite the fact that I was *not* like-minded—so that I would reap the harvest of salvation and eternal life. God specifically aligns us with those people, and we need to hear from Him clearly so we can discern who falls into the category of needing ministering or evangelizing, who falls into the fellowship category, and who simply needs to fade away from our path.

God has given me people to whom I am "assigned"—colleagues and students with whom I have relationships that started out professional but have ended up with my adding them to my list of treasured brothers and sisters in Christ. Some have become my spiritual children over the years, for whom I have been honored to pray; both parties have been blessed by these relationships. On a few occasions, my office has been converted into a sanctuary where people have felt led by the Holy Spirit to receive Christ, and we have prayed together. Why am I sharing this? Well, I want to show you how God can set the stage and how He showed me with whom to make connections because they were in it for the long haul. So always keep your "spiritual antennae" up to see with whom God wants you to partner.

A few years ago, I was working on a project for my church's youth ministry, and the area of need was in staff development. The mission was to develop the leaders who were employed at the church as well as the many volunteers who served in the youth ministry each week. My assignment was to create a workshop on self-awareness, and my ministry partner came up with an exercise. In each workshop, we would have the participants form dyads, which we would call ISI Partners. *ISI* stands for "iron sharpens iron," which is derived from Proverbs 27:17 (NIV): "As iron sharpens iron, so it is with man." Each person in the dyad would serve as an accountability partner for the other; their purpose was to check in with each other throughout the subsequent workshops to ensure that there was encouragement and "sharpening" (strengthening, making sure that each other's "iron" was like brand new and not dull). I loved the concept, and we used it in the program. I am not sure if this ISI Partner idea originated with my partner or if she had heard the term from another source, but I use it quite frequently and do not take credit for it!

I have walked with many people in my lifetime and have experienced many seasons, both good and bad. As the seasons have changed, so have the people in my circle; the roster has changed and the lineup has shifted according to what God sees are my needs in each season. There have been saints whom I believe will always be in my life here on earth (and in heaven, too—thank you, Jesus!). But even those saints may not play the same role during each season, and that is fine. For example, I used to spend a lot of time in the home of my spiritual family, the ones who brought me to Christ. Now, seventeen years later, we are still family in Christ, but I don't see them as often as I used to or would like due to commitments and balancing work, family, life, and ministry. But we still sharpen one another, and I have actually been able to sharpen *them* now that I am a more seasoned Christian. They used to be on my speed dial because I called them every time I needed prayer, and now they call upon me to pray for their needs. Only Jesus can sanctify us and mature us in that way.

My spiritual father was instrumental in helping me better understand the concept of ISI and to get the full picture of its meaning, and he probably doesn't even know that he helped me in this way. One day I sent out a mass e-mail devotional that featured Proverbs 27:17 and thanked the recipients of the e-mail for allowing me to sharpen them. "Pa" was the first to respond, and asked he me a reflective question: "Are you allowing yourself to be sharpened by others, or are you doing all of the 'sharpening'?" Sharpening is a two-way street. Are you are a sharpener who does not allow or think to have others sharpen you? Remember, a literal fellowship refers to two fellows on a ship who are rowing in the same direction and are willing to meet each other's needs so they can both get across the sea and reach their destination. This is something that I learned from a sermon preached by Bishop T.D. Jakes on his television program *The Potter's Touch*. Based on that understanding, my answer to Pa's question was no. I was pouring into others, making deposits but feeling withdrawn. That happens sometimes, especially when you have the gift of exhortation and your deepest motivation is to see others sharpened. In the process, your axe may become dull, and you may end up feeling depleted. So, I had to change my mind-set and allow others to sharpen me, too.

How do you know when you are being sharpened? Well, first, does the sharpener speak from the Word of God, or does he or she bring other, non-biblical doctrine into the mix? Does he or she compromise his or her values and beliefs and encourage you to do the same in order to do what "feels right"? Does he or she edify you, build you up to go higher, or just use you to gain height or weight in his or her own walk? Does the person make every conversation all about him- or herself? Is there a lot of taking and no giving? Granted, there will be seasons when all the focus may be on one person because he or she is going through a hardship. That person needs some serious sharpening. But if *every* season is about the other person, then how sharp can he or she make you? Does the person use wisdom when giving you counsel, or does he or she shoot from the hip and speak from a natural, carnal, and worldly perspective? When it comes to friendships and wisdom, remember Proverbs 13:20 (AMP): "He who walks [as a companion] with wise men is wise, but he who associates with [self-confident] fools is [a fool himself and] shall smart for it."

There is also a Scripture that reads, "Do not be deceived; bad company corrupts good character" (1 Cor. 15:33 NIV). And it does. When I was a "baby Christian," I was still hanging around unsaved people who were running wild. One coworker at the time advised me to move away from a crowd that I was hanging tough with because they were eventually going to bring me down. The desire of my heart was to bring them up, but that was not going to happen, as this woman warned me. There were several of them and only one of me—only one person of God, and the company was not good. Actually, most of the people with whom I walked in my early years as a Christian were not into the Lord. Their lifestyles were not in alignment with where God wanted to bring me. So, gradually, I walked away. The general consensus was that all were drinkers (heavy drinkers, I might add) and were not exactly treating their bodies as temples, as described in 1 Corinthians 6:15–20 (AMP).

> Do you not see and know that your bodies are members (bodily parts) of Christ (the Messiah)? Am I therefore to take the parts of Christ and make [them] parts of a prostitute? Never! Never! Or do you not know and realize that when a man joins himself to a prostitute, he becomes one body with her? The two, it is written, shall become one flesh. But the person who is united to the Lord becomes one spirit with Him. Shun immorality and all sexual looseness [flee from impurity in thought, word, or deed]. Any other sin which a man commits is one outside the body, but he who commits sexual immorality sins against his own body. Do you not know that your body is the temple (the

very sanctuary) of the Holy Spirit Who lives within you, Whom you have received [as a Gift] from God? You are not your own, you were bought with a price [purchased with a preciousness and paid for, made His own]. So then, honor God and bring glory to Him in your body.

I added this Scripture as a side note to remind you that every time you are tempted to "lie down" with someone and give your body to him or her, you become joined together with that person. It is very difficult to shake that person off of you when the time comes that you have to walk away. I was walking with people who were misusing their bodies with sex and alcohol, so I needed to get onto a different path in order to achieve what God had for me in that season. Their lifestyles and mine did not mesh.

God separated me from each "crewmember," but it was a gradual sanctification process. He changed the desires in my heart and, little by little, replaced those friends with others who were like-minded, those who would sharpen me in my walk with God. Eventually, as I matured in my faith, the Lord brought new saints into my life who needed to be sharpened by me, producing some serious trade-offs. Now, does that mean that I don't love the people in the old crew? No. Does that mean that I can never speak to them? No. Does that mean that all of them are ungodly? No. Does that mean that my walk is better than or greater than theirs? No. What it *does* mean is that God needed to make room for me to meet people who were more in sync with where He was taking me. God is the captain of the ship, and He is determining our direction (another "nugget" from Minister Jones.) We are on His ship, but we also need to be on the ship with people who want their lives to go in the very same direction—God-bound. That is not to say that our life goals, visions, and missions are all the same, but our love for the Lord, our hearts, and our minds need to be in one accord.

There may be certain Christians with whom you are equally yoked, and God may give you a word that the season of walking with them is over. As devastating as that is, you have to walk away—loving them and praying for them. Knowing that you were ISI Partners at one time in your life is a blessing. That person has a special place in your memory bank and in your history; God may or may not bring you back in fellowship with that person, but that is for God to determine.

I pray that your iron is being sharpened and that you allow yourself to sharpen someone else's iron, too, in order to have those relationships that are true partnerships—sharing your heart and your mind as two fellows on a ship, rowing in the same direction—in the flow of the Holy Spirit. If you are lacking in this area, if God is uprooting you from your friends, or if you are feeling alone, I pray that you will wait on the Lord as He works out the details in bringing ISI Partners into your life. If God has given you such partners for this season in your life, then brother or sister, consider yourself *blessed*.

CHAPTER 11

The Waiting Game

Have you heard of *The Dating Game*, a game show that aired in the 60s? Well, I am queen of what I call the Waiting Game. God is trying to teach me patience, how to trust Him, and how to hold out for His best. As a matter of fact, I am writing this chapter as I am waiting for my physician; I have been here for two hours, so I am trying to make the most of this Waiting Game. I used the word *game*, but quite honestly, waiting isn't really a game. I have had to find the humor in waiting and make it fun in order to keep my sanity! I have had to learn how to enjoy life while I am waiting on God's will in certain areas of my life as well as appreciate all of the blessings that I already have. As you can see, I am making productive use of my time, and God is once again putting Romans 8:28 into play for me. His allowing this divine delay is enabling me to get this book written, so God is working all things together for my good.

Although I am not the best "waiter," I have to admit that waiting on the Lord is the best thing to do. It is definitely not a good thing to jump ahead of Him if you believe that He is moving too slowly or if you have a plan that sounds better than His. Some people like to take the bull by the horns and make things happen, and some situations do call for action, as long as the Holy Spirit is prompting you to move. If you are feeling pressured to move on something and it doesn't feel right in your spirit, just "be still and know that He is God" (Ps. 46:10 NIV). God knows the exact plan and the best timing for a situation. One of my mom's cousins used to say, "When in doubt, stand still." While that doesn't sound too biblical, it may be best in a given situation. If you are experiencing apprehension about a decision, you had better stand still and seek the Lord. Waiting allows for you to call upon the Lord, pray and fast, and seek His will. Sometimes it takes a while to hear something, but eventually He will speak.

A particular critical story in the Old Testament speaks to the consequences of not waiting on the Lord for His perfect will and timing (Genesis, chapters 16–21). God had promised Abraham and Sarah that they would conceive a child and that Abraham would be the "Father of the Nations." Abraham and Sarah waited years for this promise to come to pass, and from their earthly perspectives, it looked like it was not going to happen. Sarah was getting up there in years and was still not conceiving a child, so she came up with a wild idea to have Abraham have sexual intercourse with their handmaiden, Hagar, and from there, a son was conceived and born (Ishmael). However, this was not God's will for them. They went ahead of the plan, and right after Ishmael was conceived, there was tremendous strife in that household. Years later, Sarah, at ninety years old, and Abraham, at one hundred, were able to conceive their own son, Isaac, who was the one promised by God. God waited until it was utterly impossible in the natural world for an event to happen to finally bring it to pass. From there, the Nation of Israel was born, and they were and still are God's chosen people.

Hagar and Ishmael were banished from the home as a result of the contention between Sarah and Hagar. The serious lesson in this story is to not go ahead of God's plan. A saying in one of the churches that I visit goes like this: "Do you want an Ishmael or an Isaac?" My translation is, "Do you want God's permissive will or His perfect will?" Do you want to strong-arm God, or do you want to wait for His best? Sure, some blessings may flow as a result of going ahead of God with your own plans. But God is under no obligation to bless *your* plans, so keep that in mind before you forge ahead with your own program. I have known many people who have charged ahead with their own agendas and then later were miserable, including men and women who were not peaceful about getting married but decided to go through with the ceremony and then later realized that it wasn't God's will for their lives. Although everything in our being is telling us to move forward, if that "still, small inner voice" (the Holy Spirit) is calling us back, it is imperative that we wait on the Lord until further notice.

We must wait on the Lord and continue to submit our requests to Him, waiting with expectancy (Ps. 5:3). As Luke wrote (Luke 11:9–13 AMP), "So I say to you, Ask and keep on asking and it shall be given you; seek and keep on seeking and you shall find; knock and keep on knocking and the door shall be opened to you. For everyone who asks and keeps on asking receives; and he who seeks and keeps on seeking finds; and to him who knocks and keeps on knocking, the door shall be opened. What father among you, if his son asks for a loaf of bread, will give him a stone; or if he asks for a fish, will instead of a fish give him a serpent? Or if he asks for an egg, will give him a scorpion? If you then, evil as you are, know how to give good gifts [gifts that are to their advantage] to your children, how much more will your heavenly Father give the Holy Spirit to those who ask and continue to ask Him!" In other words, keep on waiting, and keep on asking, too, while you are waiting.

I have compiled a list of all of the Scriptures within the Book of Psalms (AMP) that speak of waiting on the Lord. The Psalms were written by David, who waited years to become king and, in the meantime, was on the run from King Saul, who wanted him dead. He cried out on many occasions, and because of this, we have some of the most amazing Scriptures to comfort us when we are waiting on the Lord and when things are not looking too good. I italicized the word *wait* in each passage to emphasize it.

> Psalm 5:3—"In the morning, You hear my voice, O Lord; in the morning I prepare [a prayer, a sacrifice] for You and watch and *wait* [for You to speak to my heart]."

> Psalm 25:3—"Yes, let none who trust and *wait* hopefully and look for You be put to shame or be disappointed; let them be ashamed who forsake the right or deal treacherously without cause."

> Psalm 25:5—"Guide me in Your truth and faithfulness and teach me, for You are the God of my salvation; for You [You only and altogether] do I *wait* [expectantly] all the day long."

Psalm 25:21—"Let integrity and uprightness preserve me, for I *wait* for and expect You."

Psalm 27:11—"Teach me Your way, O Lord, and lead me in a plain and even path because of my enemies [those who lie in *wait* for me]."

Psalm 27:14—"*Wait* and hope for and expect the Lord; be brave and of good courage and let your heart be stout and enduring. Yes, *wait* for and hope for and expect the Lord."

Psalm 31:24—"Be strong and let your heart take courage, all you who *wait* for and hope for and expect the Lord!"

Psalm 33:18—"Behold, the Lord's eye is upon those who fear Him [who revere and worship Him with awe], who *wait* for Him and hope in His mercy and loving-kindness."

Psalm 33:20—"Our inner selves *wait* [earnestly] for the Lord; He is our Help and our Shield."

Psalm 33:22—"Let Your mercy and loving-kindness, O Lord, be upon us, in proportion to our *waiting* and hoping for You."

Psalm 37:7—"Be still and rest in the Lord; *wait* for Him and patiently lean yourself upon Him; fret not yourself because of him who prospers in his way, because of the man who brings wicked devices to pass."

Psalm 37:9—"For evildoers shall be cut off, but those who *wait* and hope and look for the Lord [in the end] shall inherit the earth."

Psalm 37:34—"*Wait* for and expect the Lord and keep and heed His way, and He will exalt you to inherit the land; [in the end] when the wicked are cut off, you shall see it."

Psalm 39:7—"And now, Lord, what do I *wait* for and expect? My hope and expectation are in You."

Psalm 40:1—"I *waited* patiently and expectantly for the Lord; and He inclined to me and heard my cry."

Psalm 42:5 and Psalm 43:5—"Why are you cast down, O my inner self? And why should you moan over me and be disquieted within me? Hope in God and *wait* expectantly for Him, for I shall yet praise Him, my Help and my God."

Psalm 52:9—"I will thank You and confide in You forever, because You have done it [delivered me and kept me safe]. I will *wait* on, hope in and expect in Your name, for it is good, in the presence of Your saints (Your kind and pious ones)."

Psalm 56:2—"They that lie in *wait* for me would swallow me up or trample me all day long, for they are many who fight against me, O Most High!"

Psalm 62:1—"For God alone my soul *waits* in silence; from Him comes my salvation."

Psalm 62:5—"My soul, *wait* only upon God and silently submit to Him; for my hope and expectation are from Him."

Psalm 69:3—"I am weary with my crying; my throat is parched; my eyes fail with *waiting* [hopefully] for my God."

Psalm 69:6—"Let not those who *wait* and hope and look for You, O Lord of hosts, be put to shame through me; let not those who seek and inquire for and require You [as their vital necessity] be brought to confusion and dishonor through me, O God of Israel."

Psalm 104:27—"These all *wait* and are dependent upon You, that You may give them their food in due season."

Psalm 106:13—"But they hastily forgot His works; they did not [earnestly] *wait* for His plans [to develop] regarding them."

Psalm 119:166—"I am hoping and *waiting* [eagerly] for Your salvation, O Lord, and I do Your commandments."

Psalm 130:5—"I *wait* for the Lord, I expectantly *wait*, and in His word do I hope."

Psalm 130:6—"I am looking and *waiting* for the Lord more than watchmen for the morning, I say, more than watchmen for the morning."

Psalm 145:15—"The eyes of all *wait* for You [looking, watching, and expecting] and You give them their food in due season."

Although I have entitled this chapter "The Waiting Game," I must say again that waiting is not a game; it is serious business (I was just being cute with the title of the chapter). Please wait on the Lord and don't jump ahead of Him. Become the best "waiter" that you can be, and the Lord will definitely serve you up something special. So instead of trying to strong-arm God with your plans, allow Him to make your arms stronger (as you lift them up in surrender) and wait to receive His best.

CHAPTER 12

What the Lord Really Hates

Proverbs 6:17–19 (NIV) is one of my favorite passages of Scripture. I love it because it really takes a deep look at what grieves the Lord, and some of us have been guilty of committing one (or more) of these abominable acts. Mind you, the Lord hates all sin, but this is a good Scripture to reflect on to understand what really gets "under God's skin." It reads as follows:

> There are six things the LORD hates, seven that are detestable to him: haughty eyes, a lying tongue, hands that shed innocent blood, a heart that devises wicked schemes, feet that are quick to rush into evil, a false witness who pours out lies and a person who stirs up conflict in the community.

As you read, you may have noticed some overlap in terms of what is not pleasing to God. The word *lie* comes up twice, which is also mentioned in one of the Ten Commandments given to Moses for the Israelites (Ex. 20:16 NIV): "You shall not give false testimony against your neighbor." I am sure that the majority of God's children lie on occasion, some on a daily basis, and yes, if we confess our sins to the Lord and repent, we will be pardoned. However, I don't believe we truly understand the ramifications of bearing false witness, both on ourselves and the other parties involved. A lying tongue and a false witness who pours out lies are related, so let's touch upon this issue first.

It is really tough to deal with a person who lies. Lying damages credibility and also ruins the trust between the liar and the person who is being deceived. I know two people who tend to tell "tall tales."

They have embellished and stretched the truth so much over the years that I don't believe a word that comes out of either of their mouths. I second-guess everything that they share with me, as well as any stories I hear second-hand from others who heard them from these two. I have gotten to the point that if these two individuals told me that the sky was blue and the grass was green, I would have to go outside and look for myself before taking their word for it. Lying, especially in a compulsive or pathological way (such as lying for attention), ruins one's reputation. The person will always have that label, even when telling the truth. The Lord does not like lying because it destroys relationships and can create lots of strife. I have seen long-term friendships, close family ties, even godly fellowships destroyed because of one lie that may have seemed small to one person but was major to the other. The two Scriptures are very specific, though—a "lying tongue" means that the person, most likely, isn't just telling a "white lie" or something untrue in order to shield another person from being hurt. No, this person has a lying tongue, which means that he or she lies on a regular basis; lying is a way of life for that individual. Therefore, lying is that tongue's usual state of being, and that is detestable in God's eyes. Making a living out of telling lies, or "pouring out lies," as the Scripture says, is not of God. If it is not of God, then who is the author of those lies? Our enemy, Satan, surely is! Satan uses those individuals who lie (bear false witness) in his ultimate plot to "kill, steal, and destroy" (John 10:10), so don't allow yourself to be controlled by him. Turn away from those ungodly behaviors.

Haughty eyes are the first things mentioned, so they were probably the first on God's mind when He gave Solomon this Proverb. *Haughty* is another word for *arrogant*. God hates arrogance, as do many of us! Remember that God wants us to be confident in Him and what He has given us and done for us. We can't take credit for our successes and victories, for God is the one who has blessed us. When others don't have what we have or don't live as well as we live (or don't do what we say to do), we must not look down on them, nor must we look away from them. God is the author and the finisher of our faith (Heb. 12:2 NIV), so He is the only author and finisher of our lives—all of our lives! We cannot think that we have everything under control—that's God's job! Those who look at others and think that they are "all that and then some" in comparison to those around them are not pleasing to God. In fact, God wants us to be the exact opposite, walking with a humble, meek, gentle spirit, not sizing up anyone else. *Prideful* is another word used for *haughty.* Pride is something that destroys people's spirits. Many people hold onto grudges for decades just because they are stubborn and don't want to swallow their hurt and forgive. Or they are too prideful to ask for help, not wanting to show vulnerability or inability. This is a common form of insecurity; people don't want to show their weaknesses so they act like the only things that they possess are strengths. They would rather walk around bound up in pride than be delivered, forgiving, humble, and free.

The Scripture says that those who exalt themselves will be humbled and those who humble themselves will be exalted (Matt. 23:12 KJV). As James wrote in chapter 4, verse 10 (AMP), "Humble yourselves [feeling very insignificant] in the presence of the Lord, and He will exalt you [He will lift you up and make your lives significant]." And on the heels of that Scripture, we have, "God opposes the proud but gives grace to the humble" (James 4:6 NIV). The Lord sees the lowly one and barely recognizes the one who has elevated himself. As stated in Psalm 138:6 (AMP), "For though the Lord is high, yet has He respect to the lowly [bringing them into fellowship with Him]; but the proud and haughty He knows and recognizes [only] at a distance." There is one more Scripture "for the road," from Proverbs 29:23 (AMP): "A man's pride will bring him low, but he who is of a humble spirit will obtain honor." These five Scriptures work together to really show us that pride needs to go and humility needs to show.

"Hands that shed innocent blood" is a tough point to address, so I am going to do it as delicately as I can. This pertains to harming someone as well as killing someone. The first thing that comes to my mind as I am writing this is abortion, for the blood of an unborn fetus is definitely innocent. First, I must start out by saying that I am not here to judge anyone who has sinned against God, for I sin every day, as we all do. Abortion is a very controversial issue, and it is almost an epidemic in the United States. Abortion, in God's eyes, is considered murder, although many pro-choice individuals will disagree, saying that a fetus is not a human until it is born. Let's allow God to be the judge of that since He is the one who created all of us. I know close to twenty women who have chosen to have abortions, and it is one of the most (if not *the* most) challenging positions in which a woman could ever be. I thank the Lord that I have never had to be in those shoes, and, in the name of Jesus, I would never want to wear those shoes. We must not condemn those women who have had abortions nor those who perform the actual abortion procedure; the Lord will judge, not us. He brings judgment but also mercy. I firmly believe that abortion, along with any other type of shedding of blood, is a sin that brings torment and effects that are very hard to shake. A woman can have one conviction for years (pro-life) and then find herself in a position that she considers it as an option, perhaps because of health reasons, finances, or convenience. We cannot judge the motive, validating and rationalizing one over the other. Whenever innocent blood is shed, there is something that just sits on the spirit of the one who caused the bloodshed, a feeling from which it is hard to recover. Today, I am here to reassure you that God is a forgiving Father. I want to take a moment to encourage anyone who has had an abortion, taken a life, or shed someone's blood in another fashion. Jesus' blood will cleanse you if you receive Him today; grab a hold of that truth. There are consequences to our actions, but they are for God to determine. I am not giving anyone a license to kill, nor am I justifying murder. In fact, one of the commandments given by the Lord to Moses in Exodus 20:13 (KJV) is, "Thou shall not kill." Because God is the Creator, He also dictates when the life that He created will leave this earth, not us. However, for those under the oppression of having committed such an act, I have four words for you—"Cry out to Jesus" (also a song title by Christian recording artists Third Day). Once you do, you will feel a release from that oppressive spirit that has had you in chains. And once you accept the Lord as your personal Savior, you will know that the child that was aborted is waiting for you in heaven. For those who have murdered, after you have repented to the Lord, know that if the person whose life you took was a believer in Christ, then you will embrace that person in heaven someday.

I am going to tackle the next two items together. God also hates a heart that devises wicked schemes and feet that are quick to rush into evil. Neither are of God; the Devil is the inventor of evil, and he loves it when our hearts (our motives, our agendas) are impure. There are a few people I know—and intentionally avoid—who have malice in their hearts. I truly believe that their goal in life is to be used by the Enemy to plot against people in a wicked fashion. They are not happy unless they are wishing harm on people or making up stories that will cause harm or destruction. Unfortunately, two people who are connected to me are notorious for that; these two people harbor hate in their hearts and also have wished harm, even illness, on people who are close to me. Again, would God approve of that type of behavior or emotion? Heck no, He would not! So, these two have allowed themselves to be "special agents" for the Devil. And then, there are others who run into mischief willingly and quickly (they are the "first ones in the pool") to make sure that evil takes place. They are the ones who love controversy and want to be in the middle of it. That is not of God, for the Lord wants harmony and unity.

The seventh thing that God hates is conflict (or strife, dissension) among the brethren (community, as per the NIV). This last one overlaps with the above wicked heart and evil feet, but the Scripture notes that this seventh thing is really bad. Another version of the Bible (KJV) says that it is an abomination, which is one of the worst things. Anyone whose goal it is to "stir the pot" and pit people against one another is not someone with whom you want to be involved or affiliated. It is not someone you can trust, for the person makes you think that he or she is on your side but is "playing both sides of the fence," loyal to no one. This is especially detestable when it happens in the body of Christ. As Christians, we sometimes allow that spirit of dissension (perhaps not on purpose) into our congregations; beware that Satan looks for any crack in the foundation to crawl in and start controversy. One of the most well-known examples of such an abomination was the serpent in the Garden of Eden (Genesis 3 KJV). The serpent approached Eve and stirred up strife between her and the Lord by making her question what God's command really was; that's what divisive people do. They slither in, usually disguised or camouflaged, like a wolf in sheep's clothing (Matt. 7:15 KJV), appearing very sincere but with a motive to destroy relationships. If that isn't the work of the Enemy (John 10:10), then I don't know what is!

As you can see, these seven things that God hates somewhat overlap, but the common theme is that Satan is behind most of the motives of these detestable acts. Sometimes it is our flesh that acts up; let's own it and call it what it is. God doesn't want anything in our lives that violates the Ten Commandments that He gave Moses to deliver to the Israelites, nor does He want the rest of the Word of God (Old and New Testaments) contradicted. These seven things live and breathe evil—pride, lying, falsehoods, murder, strife, division, and malice in heart and actions. I encourage you to meditate on Proverbs 6:17–19 and let it sink into your being—your heart, mind, and spirit. You don't want the Enemy to leak into any part of your life and cause you to stumble in your walk, and you don't want to have anyone who represents these things to be walking with you. Pray for wisdom and discernment to see if anyone in your life is exhibiting any of these behaviors, and, if so, ask the Lord to allow you to confront those spirits or move the people far, far away from you.

CHAPTER 13

The Most Popular Psalm

Psalm 23 is the most popular passage of Scripture in the Bible. Sometimes I think that it is more popular than John 3:16, which speaks of Jesus' coming, death, and resurrection and our salvation, our eternal gift. The reason that this psalm is so well known is that it speaks to the gentleness of our God but also to His ability to care for us, comfort us, restore us, provide for us, and protect us, all in one psalm. I want to take this Scripture line by line (again—sorry!) so you can get the full effect of it. It is commonly used in funeral services; I chose it to be written on my mom's prayer cards at the funeral home. It was a psalm that was on the tip of my tongue when the funeral director asked me what my preference was. I guess I associated it with passing and finding comfort and freedom in heaven with the Lord, but it is so much more than that. It is for the living as well as those who are enjoying paradise with the Father, Son, and Holy Spirit. Actually, it is *more* for the living than the dead. The deceased do not have to worry about their enemies or fearing evil if they are in heaven. It is a simple, yet powerful, set of verses that brings such peace. I pray that you will read and meditate on it and find that peace if you don't already possess it. Psalm 23 (KJV) reads as follows:

> The LORD is my shepherd; I shall not want. He maketh me to lie down in green pastures: he leadeth me beside the still waters. He restoreth my soul: he leadeth me in the paths of righteousness for his name's sake. Yea, though I walk through the valley of the shadow of death, I will fear no evil: for thou art with me; thy rod and thy staff they comfort me. Thou preparest a table before me in the presence of mine enemies: thou anointest my head with oil; my cup runneth over. Surely goodness and mercy shall

follow me all the days of my life: and I will dwell in the house of the LORD for ever.

For some reason, I chose the King James Version here, but I recommend that you read it in some of the other versions (especially the Amplified) to get a sense of other ways in which it is interpreted.

"The Lord is my shepherd; I shall not want" is a simple sentence with an amazing message. If you can, visualize the Lord as a great shepherd in charge of every flock of sheep. He knows how to care for His sheep, even though He has millions (if not billions) to which He tends. Because He is the shepherd, there is no want. There is nothing of which you are deprived, even if you think you are in lack. John 10:27 (NIV) says, "My sheep know my voice," so if we know the voice of this great shepherd and He knows our voices, too, then He will hear our every need. There is no lack, no want. You may think that you are in lack because there is something that you want—but not really need—and you don't have it yet. Know that the Lord provides us with what we need first and then what we desire, as long as it is in alignment with His perfect will and timing for our lives.

"He maketh me to lie down in green pastures: he leadeth me beside the still waters"; with God as our shepherd, we get to lie down like sheep do in the pastures—green pastures that are rich and vibrant. We can lie down, which means we can rest. Note that sheep are not as complex as humans are. In fact, they are some of the simplest animals alive. When David draws an analogy between sheep and us, with God being the shepherd, he is saying that we need to be simple and easygoing, like sheep. We can lie down in the pasture; we can sit by the water—not just any water, but the "still" water, which means that we need to be still as well. Worry, doubt, fear, anxiety, confusion, depression, and frustration can *go*! All of that creates chaos and shakes our peace, or our "stillness." I am just imagining myself lying in the green grass overlooking the lake, just the Lord and me. I had to take the "shepherd" and "sheep" thoughts away for the moment so I can just visualize that ultimate picture of perfection. Being by water is peaceful to me—so serene. I believe you get the picture and will agree that the Lord laying you down in the greenness of the pasture, where sheep get their yummy grass, and by the water, where they can drink, demonstrates not only peace but provision—rest, but food and drink, too. In Revelation 7:17, the apostle John confirms this: "For the Lamb at the center of the throne will be your shepherd; He will lead them to springs of living water. And God will wipe every tear from their eyes" (NIV).

"He restoreth my soul: he leadeth me in the paths of righteousness for his name's sake." God is a restorer, a healer. He takes every wrong and makes it right and is the lover of our souls. Our souls comprise our thoughts and our emotions, which trigger our behaviors. Our souls, before we were saved, really needed a cleansing. We needed the blood of Jesus to give them a good washing. However, once we are saved, we are cleansed by the blood, but we still need to be sanctified, which means, "set apart from the rest" or "made holy." The soul-cleansing, or receiving Christ, is a one-time thing, but being sanctified is a process, and restoration takes time. So God restores our souls, reassuring us that we are His, and He wants us to renew our minds and guard our hearts. I don't know about you, but I need daily reassurance that I am being restored, healed, and made whole. Isn't it refreshing to know that restoration is ours, in the name of the Lord? Righteousness is ours, too! God leads us in righteousness in the name of Jesus. We are made right with God because of what Jesus did on Calvary at the cross. God leads us down the right path daily; we just have to make sure that we follow Him on that path and take our life instruction manual (the Bible) with us, living life according to the Word. Our compass is the cross, and we need to look to that cross for our direction. Jesus carried the cross of our shame and suffering, and God leads us on this righteous path for His name's sake, which is His Son, Jesus. We are in right standing and must attempt to follow Jesus daily. We will fall down along the way, but isn't it great to know that restoration and righteousness are gifts from the shepherd?

"Yea, though I walk through the valley of the shadow of death, I will fear no evil: for thou art with me; thy rod and thy staff they comfort me." This is the verse of the Scripture that makes people, including me, think that it is associated with death and dying. But those who are living need to pay heed to this, for as we discussed in the chapter on Ephesians 6:10–17, we are in a daily spiritual battle against principalities. Therefore, we encounter the valley of the shadow of death on occasion. Satan would love nothing more than to wipe us Christians out for we are a threat to the kingdom of darkness. Sometimes we don't even know the death and destruction from which God has blocked us, that was waiting for us to turn the corner. God has turned so many things around for us, and we don't even know the half of it. We must fear no evil because God is with us, carrying all the weapons that we need, and our battle gear is on. From a shepherd-and-sheep perspective, taking this Scripture literally, the shepherd has a rod and a staff to keep any of his flock from going astray. The last thing a shepherd wants is to have hunters capturing or shooting the sheep in order to make lamb chops, or perhaps a nice sheepskin coat or a few sweaters for Christmas. A shepherd is not going to let anyone steal or shoot any of his flock (refer to Matt. 18:12–14 NIV). So, if a shepherd feels that way about an animal, how much more does God feel about His children, the saints? God is not going to let anyone kill, steal, or destroy us. We are His; He will protect us and bring comfort, so we don't have to be afraid. We may be under attack—God allows attacks so that we can cling to Him and trust Him to provide, protect, and comfort us. We can run for cover under His mighty wing, or under his rod and staff!

"Thou preparest a table before me in the presence of mine enemies: thou anointest my head with oil; my cup runneth over." Isn't it just like God to set up a banquet table for us, right smack in the middle of those who have come against us? Well, He does that because He is a just God and wants to show those who mess with His "kiddies" that we are joyous, that we have overcome, and that the Lord will prevail. He anoints us with oil as a seal of His love (symbolic of healing) and protection. Our cup runs over, which, again, means that we shall not be in lack but will be prosperous. In fact, we will have life and have it more abundantly (John 10:10).

I remember a time in my life when I had a personal issue and everyone I thought was a friend was talking a whole lot of junk about me. I was being mocked behind my back, but to my face, people were smiling and being phony. It was a few years after I came to the Lord, and I was so humiliated about an incident that happened in a nightclub between me and a guy I had dated and his new girlfriend. We were "over" but he didn't seem to think so, and he was trying to have "his cake and eat it, too". The story became so convoluted that it resembled the telephone game that we used to play as children. By the time the story circled back to me, it was completely different than what had actually happened. In fact, by that point, I was being portrayed as having a drinking problem, causing scenes in nightclubs, and practically being a home wrecker. Nothing could have been further from the truth! Two other people who were involved in the incident believed me over the entire "he said, she said" group of gossipmongers, but the Lord put a gag order on me; He didn't want me to try to clear my reputation with all of the others. It was really difficult for me not to defend myself, especially against things that weren't even true! God wanted me to wait, leave it in His hands, and trust that He would bring justice (and vengeance, too). A few weeks later, I heard that those who had been part of the gossip circle that wagged their tongues with lies about me had begun to experience hardships in their lives—one by one over the course of the next few months. I hadn't wished harm on anyone and so wasn't pleased with what was happening, but I knew that it was the Lord preparing a table for me in the presence of my enemies. As the *chismosos* (Spanish for "gossipers") were suffering in their trials, God brought me a brand new relationship, a promotion at work, and a walk with the Lord that was growing stronger, and the joy of the Lord was my strength (Neh. 8:10 NIV). While I was feasting at the banquet table, my enemies were eating my crumbs! God prepared a table for me in their presence and anointed me with the oil of healing and praise, and I was living the life while they were drowning. Again, I didn't rejoice over their misfortune, but I did see God's hand in it all. I moved on to another job about a year and a half later, where God really "opened the floodgates of heaven" and poured out many blessings by elevating me to the position for which I had been waiting almost four years. My cup was running over and spilling on me, but I welcomed those stains with open arms.

"Surely goodness and mercy shall follow me all the days of my life: and I will dwell in the house of the LORD forever." What can I say about this passage? With goodness and mercy following me, I will be the leader any day! And they will follow me all the days of my life, too? Even better! I need all the mercy I can get, and goodness, too. That I will dwell in the house of the Lord all the days of my life is a promise that's so reassuring.

The gist of this psalm is captured in the following poem that the Lord just gave me:

> Basking in His presence,
> always under His care,
> striving for God's best each day on earth,
> preparing for our Eternal Affair!

CHAPTER 14

Why Am I Here?

Have you ever thought, *Why am I here?* or *What is my purpose on this earth?* Well, Rick Warren, senior pastor at the Saddleback Church in California, wrote a book entitled *The Purpose-Driven Life* (Zondervan, 2002). Warren does an outstanding job of outlining God's purpose for our lives, breaking it down into five categories and providing daily reflections for a forty-day period. It is a must that you read this anointed yet practical book; it will give you an enlightened perspective as to why you are here and how, as a believer in Christ, you are called to live. I suggest that those of you who have already read it reread it after you have read this book to give yourself a "refresher course" on your purpose.

I want us to read a very important Scripture and keep it in mind as we progress through the chapter. I quoted it previously, but it is worth a second showing. It is Jeremiah 1:5 (KJV): "Before I formed thee in the belly I knew thee; and before thou camest forth out of the womb I sanctified thee, and I ordained thee a prophet unto the nations." I had read this Scripture before and understood it. However, it was one of the Scriptures with which Dr. Bond opened up her sermon the day she prophesied about the book that I was to write, the book that you are now reading. I will always remember her delivery of this passage, as well as her connection of it to the first chapter of Genesis—the beginning of time and the beginning of the earth. God knew you before time began. He had you in mind even as He was creating the sun, the moon, the stars, the seas, the animals and all living things, and humans. So you are not a mistake, an accident, or a surprise to God. He is the master architect, and He had the blueprint of you designed long before you were even a thought in your mother's or father's mind. For those who started out in life without a mom or a dad; whose parents abandoned them along the way; or who are feeling worthless, full of guilt and shame, there is a promise in Psalm 27:10, which reads, "Though my mother and father forsake me, the Lord will receive me" (NIV). If you do not have an earthly mom or dad, or if you do not have a good relationship with your earthly parents, rejoice in the fact that you have a heavenly Father who is so crazy about you, so wild about you, that He knows you from the inside out and wants you to get to know Him in that way, too. That is the main reason you were created—to know God and to love Him.

Jeremiah was given another word from the Lord, recorded in 29:11 (another common Scripture): "For I know the plans I have for you, says the Lord. Plans to prosper you and not to harm you, plans to give you hope and a future" (NIV). God wants us to move forward in life and to be successful; our Father has big plans for His children. Just as my parents had a plan for my life and the lives of my siblings, which required many sacrifices, my heavenly Father has even bigger and better plans for me! I believe that He has taken my parents' plans and made them a foundation for what He has in store for my future. For example, my mother lived in public housing almost all of her life with her immediate family and then moved into a larger apartment with my dad to raise us years later. My parents' intention was for Mama Cruz to be home raising us while Papa Cruz worked. She went back to work when we were in high school to help out with expenses because things were getting more costly. They never owned a home because of the expenses that homeowners incur; they believed it was more important to invest in private elementary and secondary school education for all three of their children. What a sacrifice, right? I do believe that the elementary school education that I received in my earlier years paved the way for me to write and speak the way I do (of course, my parents influenced me, too). And that is why I was successful from grade school to graduate school. I have had the good fortune to study at two private universities for my undergraduate and graduate degrees. God willing, I will be heading back to school again for a doctoral degree, but the point of this illustration is that my parents' plan for me was just a piece of the plan that God has for me. God's plans are never "small potatoes." I can't even fathom what is in store as I am walking with Him.

As I mentioned in the Introduction, I come from a diverse background of ethnicities. I love that God formed me in my mom's womb with a purpose to be so different, so unique. But I have to be honest—I haven't always loved or embraced who God created me to be. There was an incident that really changed my life and also changed my mind-set; it caused in me what the senior pastor of our church calls a paradigm shift. In 2006, I attended a multicultural women's conference. I had attended this conference three previous times, and I always enjoyed the speakers and the issues that were presented regarding the challenges that women and people of color face in the workplace and society in general. At the 2006 conference, the theme was "Authenticity," which means "truth, realness, and genuineness". At prior conferences, there was a session in which all of the women were divided into their racial groups and given a set of questions to answer within their groups. Then, they would present the themes that they discovered to the larger group when we would reconvene later in the day. During the previous years' conferences, I went with the Latina group, but for some reason, that particular year, I felt in my spirit that I needed to go with the mixed-race group. I believe that the reason my spirit was tugging at me to go to the much smaller, less popular group was because of the theme of the conference. If the speakers were presenting on authenticity, then why wouldn't I be true to who I am, to who God has created me to be, and represent my heritage in the mixed-race group?

Well, I went to the new group and found that it had only fifteen other women in it, as opposed to the Latina group, which had over two hundred. The Lord spoke to me, and when we reconvened to the larger group, I came as a different woman. I came back not just as a Latina but as someone who was truly owning who God had created her to be—a biracial (Latina/Caucasian), multicultural (Puerto Rican, Spanish, Italian, Eastern European-Jewish), American-born woman who was raised Roman Catholic and became a born-again Christian. I saw that in those previous conferences, I had been denying my mother, who is of Caucasian descent, when I was gathering with the Latina group, something that I did unintentionally.

After this experience—it was more like an encounter with the Lord, I should say—I sensed freedom and true acceptance of who God created me to be, embracing my entire makeup. There is uniqueness about each one of us. Now tell me, do you know anyone who falls into that combination of categories that I just mentioned, that mixed bag of ethnic groups? Most likely, the answer is no. My siblings do, but they are still not me. Therefore, no one is me, and wouldn't be even if I had a twin, for I am fearfully and wonderfully made (Ps. 139:14 NIV). When God created me, He broke the mold and didn't make a clone. I am a one-and-only special, and, in my thirties, I finally accepted it—better late than never, I say!

Growing up, I always tried to fit in. I frequently felt like I had to "choose" an ethnicity in order to conform to whichever group I was associated with at a given time. But recently, God gave me a Scripture and allowed me to see its meaning differently, as it pertained to my situation, bringing freedom in Christ as I connected with people for the purposes of winning souls while also embracing every aspect of myself. Through being multicultural and biracial, God has given me a special gift of understanding and embracing others' cultures in order to relate to them and build the bridge for them to Jesus, which is one of my ministries.

> Though I am free and belong to no one, I have made myself a slave to everyone, to win as many as possible. To the Jews I became like a Jew, to win the Jews. To those under the law I became like one under the law (though I myself am not under the law), so as to win those under the law. To those not having the law I became like one not having the law (though I am not free from God's law but am under Christ's law), so as to win those not having the law. To the weak I became weak, to win the weak. I have become all things to all people so that by all possible means I might save some. I do all this for the sake of the gospel that I may share in its blessings. (1 Cor. 9:19–23 NIV)

God had a plan and a purpose for me (as a "human combination platter," as I like to call myself). He knew what He was doing when He allowed my grandparents to marry and then my parents. He makes no mistakes. He knows every hair on my head (Luke 12:7 NIV). He knows the good, the bad, the ugly, and the pretty about me. And I am here to love Him, have fellowship with Him, and embrace myself as well as those around me, loving them and not their sins. The most important reason that He created me and each and every person on the planet—past, present, and future—is to serve His people, using our gifts and talents in a godly fashion.

So spend some time with the Lord to hear from Him what your specific purpose is on this earth and then gear up to fulfill that calling on your life!

CHAPTER 15

Trading in Our Sorrows

The Spirit of the Lord God is upon me, because the Lord has anointed and qualified me to preach the Gospel of good tidings to the meek, the poor, and afflicted; He has sent me to bind up and heal the brokenhearted, to proclaim liberty to the [physical and spiritual] captives and the opening of the prison and of the eyes to those who are bound, to proclaim the acceptable year of the Lord [the year of His favor] and the day of vengeance of our God, to comfort all who mourn, to grant [consolation and joy] to those who mourn in Zion—to give them an ornament (a garland or diadem) of beauty instead of ashes, the oil of joy instead of mourning, the garment [expressive] of praise instead of a heavy, burdened, and failing spirit—that they may be called oaks of righteousness [lofty, strong, and magnificent, distinguished for uprightness, justice, and right standing with God], the planting of the Lord, that He may be glorified.... Instead of your [former] shame you shall have a twofold recompense; instead of dishonor and reproach [your people] shall rejoice in their portion. Therefore in their land they shall possess double [what they had forfeited]; everlasting joy shall be theirs. For I the Lord love justice; I hate robbery and wrong with violence or a burnt offering. And I will faithfully give them their recompense in truth, and I will make an everlasting covenant or league with them." (Isa. 61:1–3, 7–8 AMP)

Isaiah 61 is one of my favorite chapters in the Bible. It has been near and dear to my heart, especially verse 3, for I strive each day to remember that crown of beauty, the oil of joy, and the garment of praise that I have already been given but sometimes forget to wear. We must hold onto these promises that the prophet Isaiah was given by God to tell the Israelites that Jesus was coming and that Jesus' ministry would be launched with this particular Scripture (Luke 4:18–19 NIV). The entire chapter of Isaiah 61 is worth reading, but I will outline verses 1–3 and 7–8 for you, as I did with the Lord's Prayer, Ephesians 6:10–17, Proverbs 6:17–19, and Psalm 23.

"The Spirit of the Lord God is upon me, because the Lord has anointed and qualified me to preach the Gospel of good tidings to the meek, the poor, and afflicted; He has sent me to bind up and heal the brokenhearted, to proclaim liberty to the [physical and spiritual] captives and the opening of the prison and of the eyes to those who are bound" (verse 1) is the first portion of this passage of Scripture. Jesus spoke this to His disciples, and it was a prophetic word given to Isaiah about the coming of the Messiah. Jesus' primary mission was to come to the earth as a man, but as the Son of God simultaneously, to "set captives free," which means all man, for everyone is in need of a Savior. Jesus especially came to preach the Word of God to the poor, meek, wounded, and brokenhearted (in mind, heart, spirit, soul, and body); and those who were captive, both literally (prisoners) and figuratively (from a spiritual perspective, those who were in bondage, afflicted by strongholds). Basically, Jesus came for you and me! He came, lived, ministered, died, was buried, and was resurrected in order for us to be free. So why are we still living in chains? Why are we still oppressed? We have to take hold of this Scripture and make it ours. In the hymn "All the Way to Calvary," there is a line that goes, "All the way to Calvary He went for me. He died to set me free."

This reminds me of the time when a friend, who is a Christian, and I went to visit her sister-in-law in prison. On the way there, I was a bit nervous because I didn't know what to expect. She had been in jail for over twenty years, so I thought we would be encountering a very hostile, bitter, and aggressive woman. When we entered the correctional facility, I was jittery; it was my first time in such a place, so I had to get myself situated. When the officer brought Rae, my friend's sister-in-law out to us, I saw the joy of the Lord radiating from her. Her countenance was so peaceful. She was so happy to see my friend and excited to meet me, a new friend. We spent hours with her, prayed for her before we left, and visited her a few more times throughout her time there. I wanted to cry that first time, and even as I write this, I am getting a little teary-eyed. It felt great meeting her and, more important, it was great to fellowship with both of them. Rae had come to know the Lord in prison by watching Christian programming on television whenever she was allowed to see it in the prison recreation room. But what I was really so emotional about were two things. First, I realized that I had been stereotyping all prison inmates as angry, rough, and hard. That was *not* the case with Rae. Second, she was more carefree than I was, and she has been in prison for her entire adult life, since she was eighteen years old. She didn't have the freedoms that I have, yet I was walking around with so many burdens on my mind and heart, while she was stuck in a facility and was light and breezy in her spirit. I am sharing this to show you that we can be free but be in a worse prison in our minds and hearts than actual inmates. I know people who are so "oppressed" that they are prisoners in their minds and isolate themselves from the world. That is worse than being in an actual jail cell, for you have freedom but shut yourself off from it. The lesson to remember here is that, regardless of whether you are in a physical or a psychological prison, Jesus came to set the captives, *all* captives, free! So let's not let His resurrection and our salvation be in vain.

"To proclaim the acceptable year of the Lord [the year of His favor] and the day of vengeance of our God, to comfort all who mourn" (verse 2), and "To grant [consolation and joy] to those who mourn in Zion—to give them an ornament (a garland or diadem) of beauty instead of ashes, the oil of joy instead of mourning, the garment [expressive] of praise instead of a heavy, burdened, and failing spirit" (verse 3) are the next two passages, and, as I mentioned, I am holding onto them for dear life these days. A year of favor—I will take it! How about a lifetime of favor? I know I am greedy, but because we are God's children, we can ask for daily favor, not just yearly. There will be a day of vengeance, so all of what the Enemy has stolen from you will be returned to you and the Lord will be your vindicator.

Another key Scripture for me, which, in a way "marries" this verse, is Joel 2:25 (NIV). It reads, "I will repay you for the years that the locusts have eaten—the great locust and the young locust, the other locusts and the locust swarm." A locust is a type of grasshopper that can devastate crops in a field or orchard. I always wondered why the Lord, through Joel, would go on and on about locusts—great, young, other, and a swarm. What was that all about? Well, what Joel was saying is that the Enemy will use these destructive creatures to destroy your "fruit," your livelihood, if you are not careful with your "crop" or "harvest." Joel gave us four different examples of locusts, which means that the Devil can use anything, at any age and from any category; it doesn't matter. He can use young locusts (the youth), great locusts (which could be older people or people who we think are great, even fellow Christians), other locusts (sometimes even family members), and a locust swarm (a "gang" of people, all coming at you at the same time). The great news of Joel 2:25 and Isaiah 61 (verse 3) is that God *restores* the years that were eaten away by all those pesky "locusts" and gives us a crown of beauty, oil of joy, and a garment of praise. We just have to wait on the Lord for His perfect timing. And we have to trade in our ashes, the heaviness, the burdens, and the hurt, which is sometimes hard to do, especially when it is easier to have a pity party than a praise party. Israel Houghton and his group New Breed sing a song by Darrell Evans that is sung in worship services across the nation every Sunday. Some of the lyrics are "I'm trading my sorrow, I'm trading my shame, and I'm laying it down for the joy of the Lord. I'm trading my sickness, I'm trading my pain, and I'm laying it down for the joy of the Lord. Yes, Lord, yes, Lord. Yes, yes, Lord. Amen." End of story. We have to lay it all down for the joy of the Lord.

"That they may be called oaks of righteousness [lofty, strong, and magnificent, distinguished for uprightness, justice, and right standing with God], the planting of the Lord, that He may be glorified" is the second part of verse 3. An oak is a type of tree, so the Lord is basically saying that we will be standing strong and tall, having many branches, which means that we will be fruitful with many "offshoots," or, in our case, offspring for generations to come. If we are "oaks of righteousness," we are set apart from others, representing the Lord and receiving His favor and blessings so that He may be glorified in it all. If we are representing the Lord, then we can't be shabby, walking in gloom and doom. We have to stand upright—physically, emotionally, psychologically, and most important, spiritually—so they will know us by what we are producing, by our "fruit" (Matt. 7:16 KJV).

"Instead of your [former] shame you shall have a twofold recompense; instead of dishonor and reproach [your people] shall rejoice in their portion. Therefore in their land they shall possess double [what they had forfeited]; everlasting joy shall be theirs" (verse 7) is the next verse that we are going to cover. I have heard world-renowned author, preacher, and televangelist Joyce Meyer speak on TV and also live at three of her national conferences, and on many occasions she has said that God will give you "double for your trouble." That is so true; God will give you more than you lost. You can trade in your sorrows (guilt, shame, disgrace, dishonor, loss, and so on) for sunshine, but it doesn't always come right away; you have to wait until the storm is over. Just look at the life of Job, who lost all of his children and his livestock, and afterward he was covered with boils from head to toe. His wife told him to "curse God and die" (Job 2:9 NIV). But he did not do so. Because of this, at the end of his saga, in his older age, God gave him more children, gave him more riches, and restored his health. He was blessed. Now, losing any child is a major devastation, especially losing all of them at the same time to a destructive wind that blowing into town. Having all of your animals destroyed, too, is a major blow, not because they are domestic pets like you and I may have but because that was how Job earned a living, and he was living large. Then, to be struck with ugly, painful bumps all over your body is what some may consider the final strike—"three strikes and you're out." I would have thrown in the towel right on the spot. But Job professed that the "Lord giveth and the Lord taketh away" (Job 1:21 KJV), which means to me that he understood that there will be seasons of feast and growth and then seasons of famine and loss, just as is written in Ecclesiastes 3:1–18 (NIV).

I call my grandmother a "modern-day Job." I have to share her testimony in order to clearly illustrate the different seasons in our lives and how God will bring restoration, the "beauty for the ashes." Granny lost her husband suddenly of a heart attack when she was fifty-two, after thirty years of marriage. A month later, her father died; and her mom had died years before, when Granny was in her thirties. So she was left without a mother, a father, or a husband at the young age of fifty-two. Less than two years later, her twenty-seven-year-old daughter (my aunt), a mother of two young sons, collapsed and died of a heart attack. Devastated, Granny quit her job and stepped in to help her son-in-law raise the two boys. Life settled a bit for her, and some years later, Granny met a nice man who became her companion. However, in 1978, she was diagnosed with breast cancer and had to have a mastectomy. She bounced back from that battle with radiation and the Lord's grace. In 1989, Granny experienced another blow when her only son, my uncle, died of bone cancer at age forty-eight. Shortly thereafter, each of my grandmother's siblings died, practically at the rate of one sibling per year. Over the course of the next two decades, my grandmother lost friends to old age and health-related issues, including that companion who, by that time, had been in her life for twenty years. She also developed macular degeneration (loss of sight) and loss of hearing in both ears. Four years ago, she was near death with pneumonia and failing (septic) kidneys. But God kept her and healed her, which was deemed "miraculous" by the doctors and nurses.

Today, Granny is "still standing", which is unbelievable! Then, what we thought would be the "straw that broke the camel's back" was when my mother died of a heart attack almost two years ago, brought on by heart complications related to diabetes. All three of my Granny's children had died, which was something she never thought she would live to experience. My grandmother handled it the best way she could, with God's grace yet again. After my mom's death, and with Granny's consent, my family decided that placing her in a nursing facility would be the best scenario for her now, as she would have people to watch her around the clock and would feel safe. So she left her apartment and the neighborhood that she had called home for sixty years and moved into the facility, which is near the family. Even though this totally took away her independence, she dug in her heels and accepted it, moving forward with God's grace one more time. Recently, she has had a series of bouts with infection, depression, and fatigue, and she had to be rehabilitated with physical therapy. But God still has her here and is keeping her, again. However, she is now battling lung complications related to a resurfacing of the breast cancer that she had in 1978. Granny's feisty spirit is calming down, and she is slowly surrendering to the Lord, getting ready to be with Him. She hasn't lost her faith, but she wants to know why the Lord hasn't taken her yet and why she has suffered along the way. Once God finally does take her home, she can have eternal "face time" with Him and ask Him directly all of the questions that she has. The most special thing about Granny is that she accepted Jesus Christ in her heart as the Lord of her life recently, at age ninety-five (hallelujah!). So for those of you who are praying for your loved ones to be born again, continue to stand in the gap and pray for them because the Lord will answer. You are never too old to be reborn!

When you hear my grandmother's testimony, you hear about lots of ashes, lots of mourning, and lots of heaviness. So where is the beauty? Where is the oil of gladness and the garment of praise? Where is the double portion and the everlasting joy? Well, for years, I have been asking the Lord to show me so that I could minister to her. I have to be honest—I have come up empty on many occasions. But since she has been ill lately, I have been in prayer about it again, and God has been speaking to me about what the blessings have been—the double portions. My grandmother, to me, is a legend, and not in the Hollywood celebrity sense. She will be leaving a legacy of someone who hung in there and never gave up the fight. She was a widow at a young age and never remarried, although God blessed her with a nice companion in her early senior years. Granny has also been spending many of her later years as the sole survivor of her first two immediate families—the family that she had as a child growing up in Williamsburg, Brooklyn (her parents and siblings), and the family that she and her husband raised (three children, all now deceased). She has been holding down the fort for many decades, being an inspiration to family, friends, coworkers, and now the residents with whom she lives.

The beauty among all of the ashes is that Granny had thirty really good years with my grandfather. He was a blessing in her life, giving her the attention that she needed and may not have gotten growing up as the middle child of nine in a large, Italian, immigrant family. Granny, in turn, gave him a passageway to Christ, for he was of Jewish faith and did not know Jesus until they met. Although he did not abandon his own culture and traditions, he embraced the Christian faith on many occasions, and I do hope that he personally met the Savior on his life's journey.

Granny lost her children along the way but had many good years with them as they grew up and still has lots of wonderful and funny stories. Granny has been and still is a blessing to the grandchildren who lost their parents, especially my aunt's children, who lost their mom at such as early age. She also served many of her siblings in their seasons of illness, as well as every friend and her companion, who had Alzheimer's. Seven years ago, my mom, my sister, and I stepped in to care for her, which was a major challenge in all four of our lives because Granny has a very strong and challenging personality. We were able to be there for her just as she had been there for everyone else in her younger years. My grandmother has been blessed with grandchildren, great-grandchildren, and several nieces and nephews who check in with her, and she was also a help to the other residents at the nursing facility before she took ill. She is admired by many and still looks pretty darn good at ninety-five! Her health held up for ninety-five years, for the most part, and her mind is still intact, which is more than I can say for many of her fellow residents who suffer from Alzheimer's and dementia.

The rich heritage, memories, family, friends, servant hood coupled with the fact that she is definitely a survivor is the "Trophy of Grace" that God has allowed her to be—on display for all those who know her, as well as for all those who read this book. I believe that God will have the biggest homecoming waiting for her, along with the family and friends who will be waiting for her in heaven when it is finally her time to go. My consolation for all of the suffering in her life, in a nutshell, is what is written in the following two Scriptures: Matthew 5:4 (AMP)—"Blessed and enviably happy [with a happiness produced by the experience of God's favor and especially conditioned by the revelation of His matchless grace] are those who mourn, for they shall be comforted!" and Psalm 147:3 (AMP)—"He heals the brokenhearted and binds up their wounds [curing their pains and their sorrows]." When people hear my Granny's story, they cannot believe that she is still standing. I asked her three times one day in the nursing home if she was angry or bitter with God for taking her husband and her children, and she answered no. I was glad to hear that she did not harbor either in her heart, and I know that it is only God who has given her the grace to heal her broken heart and move forward day by day.

We will miss Elvera Lucy Di Conza Goldstein tremendously when she goes, but our loss will truly be heaven's gain. Earth will not be the same without her as heaven makes room for one more saint. As Matthew

25:23 (NIV) states, "His master replied, 'Well done, good and faithful servant! You have been faithful with a few things; I will put you in charge of many things. Come and share your master's happiness'!"

Finally, verse 8 reads, "For I the Lord love justice; I hate robbery and wrong with violence or a burnt offering. And I will faithfully give them their recompense in truth, and I will make an everlasting covenant or league with them." The Lord hates when the locusts eat away at the crops, when Satan robs from us, or when any harm is done to His kids. God is a just God, and He is faithful to give us double for our trouble. We are in an eternal covenant with Him as His children.

Please read the entire Psalm 61 and let the truth of the passages sink in. This Scripture brings such freedom, joy, peace, healing, comfort, favor, restoration, justice, and righteousness—all of the above. What an awesome Father He is to His children!

Thank you for allowing me to share my heart as well as speak on behalf of Granny, who is a strong woman with a testimony that I pray touches many hearts but also serves as a lesson for those who want to give up. As we go into the next chapter, I pray that you continue your walk with Jesus with Granny's determination, along with God's grace, and that you don't give up the fight.

CHAPTER 16

Don't Give Up the Fight

In the previous chapter, I shared my grandmother's testimony. Granny is a survivor; she has earned that title because she hasn't given up the fight (reminding me of a Bob Marley song—here I go again!). It is so easy to grow weary and decide to quit before we get to the finish line. As declared in Hebrews 12:1–2 (NIV), "Therefore, since we are surrounded by such a great cloud of witnesses, let us throw off everything that hinders and the sin that so easily entangles. And let us run with perseverance the race marked out for us, fixing our eyes on Jesus, the pioneer and perfecter of faith. For the joy set before him he endured the cross, scorning its shame, and sat down at the right hand of the throne of God." We have to keep running that race and be able to say the following at the end, as stated in 2 Timothy 4:7 (NIV): "I have fought the good fight, I have finished the race, and I have kept the faith."

I have to pay tribute here to my grandparents and even my great-grandparents, who are my family's legacy. These folks who came before my parents and my generation showed us how to give to and serve others. They always had loads of people in their homes, feeding them, sometimes financially providing for them if someone was in a bind, and doing favors for people within and outside of the family. My grandfather (Papa Cruz's father) was so generous that when he left Puerto Rico back in the early 50s to come to New York to start a new life for his family, he turned over a deed to land that he owned down there to a friend, saying that the friend could have it because he wasn't going back. He was the type of man who thought nothing of giving his last dollar to a friend in need. I definitely see that quality in my father, the gift of service, as Papa Cruz has gone out of the way to help people and has given financially whenever he can help someone out of a jam. Mama Cruz was the same way—giving (her strongest spiritual gift), serving, and encouraging others. Even when she was not feeling well, she always wanted others to be blessed.

My siblings and I have inherited those attributes, along with similar spiritual gifts that God has bestowed upon us as believers in Christ. We are blessed to be in a bloodline of givers and servants on both sides of the family, and, in turn, we have been a blessing to others. However, I have to admit that I have grown weary in giving, serving, encouraging, praying for, and praying with others, especially over the past couple of years. I know that God is pleased with me when I obey Him, when I get over myself and lift someone else up out of a rut. But it's not easy. In fact, we are living in End Times, and people are generally very selfish; everyone is too busy, and sometimes ungrateful, and it annoys the living heck out of me when I take the time to be there for someone and my efforts are not appreciated or acknowledged. And then, sometimes, when I have a need, there are very few people around to help meet that need or to encourage me in the process.

The Lord spoke to me (in my spirit, not my ear) and said, "What do you think I go through?" This was a profound and challenging question for Him to ask me. If I get into a pity party or a gripe session about how slighted I feel, how does God feel when mankind, in our humanness, overlooks Him, not thanking or acknowledging what He has done for us? Jesus died to set the world free, *everyone* in the world. Who could "out-give" Jesus? No one can! No matter what amount of money you give, it will not outdo the eternal gift of salvation. Even with this amazing, eternal, life-changing gift available for all of mankind, millions of people don't even believe that Jesus is who He said He was. They are waiting for the Messiah to come or think that Jesus was a great teacher and prophet but not the Son of God. Then, there are others who don't even believe that there is a God, let alone someone we can claim as "Abba Father," and the concept of a Savior, Jesus, is a fairy tale to them. On the other end of the spectrum are many who claim to believe in Jesus but only bother with Him when they have a pressing need ("using" Him), not walking with Him, not loving Him, and not being grateful to Him, let alone serving Him. God knows our frustrations even better than we do, and He is not affected by them. God does not get frustrated, even though His Spirit is grieved by the behaviors of the world. He knows we are human and that we get caught up in our weariness of doing good for others, and God knows we feel discouraged when we "pour out" and don't get much in return. That is why He gave Isaiah this word: "But those who hope in the LORD will renew their strength. They will soar on wings like eagles; they will run and not grow weary, they will walk and not be faint" (Isa. 40:31 NIV). We need to continue to hope in the Lord and turn to Him every time we get discouraged and want to get "in the flesh" to give up the fight and abandon our faith.

Jesus also spoke to the disciples and ministered to the people, knowing they would benefit from this particular promise in Matthew 11:28–30 (NIV), saying "Come to me, all you who are weary and burdened, and I will give you rest. Take my yoke upon you and learn from me, for I am gentle and humble in heart, and you will find rest for your souls. For my yoke is easy and my burden is light." That Scripture screamed the loudest at me during the five years that my mom, sister, and I were spending nights at Granny's apartment with her. We were all crazy weary of the whole process—disgusted with her law-breaking neighbors, losing sleep from their "disturbing the peace," and then having to get through the next day despite being so tired. My mom's health was not the best and was getting worse, and this aggravating situation was not helping. My sister was raising my niece during the day while her husband worked, so the next day, there was no time for her to nap or have time to be cranky due to a lack of sleep because she had an infant and then a toddler to care for. I had a job to go to, and I would come in with *maletas* (Spanish for "suitcases") under my eyes because I was not well rested. Did we complain? Yes! Every chance we had. (I know I did, and my sister, too, but Mama Cruz kept it all in.) Regardless, God would put this Scripture on people's hearts to recite to me whenever I would start a pity party about how done I was. I learned how to pray more and draw closer to God *because of* my weariness. I had to renew my strength, get some rest (and God provided naps every now and then), change my attitude daily, and ask God to go easy on me, knowing that He is gentle and humble and His yoke is light. He was with me every time I felt weary, every time I wanted to cry. Every time I didn't want to help out anymore,

God sent one of the saints to drop a Scripture on me, give me a word of encouragement, say that they were praying for me, and give me some prophetic words and revelations during that tough season. It's a new season now with Granny, especially since my mom died, and we are experiencing a different kind of weariness (as well as healing from a state of mourning), but Matthew 11:28–30 still sustains us!

Paul spoke to the Galatians (6:7–10 NIV) and presented to them the laws of sowing and reaping, which are also related to not growing weary and continuing to sow good seeds to reap a harvest. The passage reads, "Do not be deceived: God cannot be mocked. A man reaps what he sows. Whoever sows to please their flesh, from the flesh will reap destruction; whoever sows to please the Spirit, from the Spirit will reap eternal life. Let us not become weary in doing good, for at the proper time we will reap a harvest if we do not give up. Therefore, as we have opportunity, let us do good to all people, especially to those who belong to the family of believers." In other words, if we sow apple seeds into the ground, we can't expect to produce oranges when harvest time comes. We are going to get exactly what we planted. We can't mock God, plant what we want to plant, and then think we are going to get different results. We also can't wave the white flag of surrender every time we get sluggish in sowing; we must persevere and sow the seeds that God wants us to plant so that we can produce what He wants us to have (blessing upon blessing, reward upon reward). If we plant what we, the flesh, and what the Enemy and the world say is best to sow, then we will produce a bad crop during harvest time, reaping all that is destructive to us in the long run. We have to continue to plant good seeds for all, especially those who are ambassadors for Christ, representing their faith. Don't grow weary in sowing, because in due season, you will reap the harvest. There is a lot of time between planting and producing, sowing and reaping—ask any farmer. Therefore, we will have to wait to see great results (refer back to the chapter "The Waiting Game").

So, my friends, running the race is not easy. It takes stamina, perseverance, and grace, and it grows the fruit of the spirit, as detailed in Galatians 5:22–23 (NIV): "But the fruit of the Spirit is love, joy, peace, forbearance, kindness, goodness, faithfulness, gentleness and self-control." It also takes us putting our trust in the Lord and holding onto these key Scriptures so that we don't lose heart, lose faith, or lose our minds as we cross the finish line. So hold onto the One who is going to make it all right. Don't lose hope, and don't give up the fight!

CHAPTER 17

Bless Me, Keep Me, Move Me, Free Me

Bruce Wilkinson wrote a great book that sold millions of copies and made *The New York Times* best-seller list. It was a little book, an easy read, called *The Prayer of Jabez* (Multnomah Books, 2000) and was based on 1 Chronicles 4:10. Jabez was a man in the Old Testament who was a descendant of Judah, born to his mother with lots of pain during labor. She was in so much pain during this birth that she named him Jabez, which translates to "pain." Wow! Can you imagine being named Pain? With this, I must say that we need to be mindful of what we name our children.

The simple passage of Scripture reads as follows: "Jabez cried out to the God of Israel, 'Oh that you would bless me and enlarge my territory! Let your hand be with me, and keep me from harm so that I will be free from pain.' And God granted his request" (1 Chron. 4:10 NIV).

Jabez cried out to the Lord because he wanted to be blessed, not walk around with a name that reminds himself and others of pain. We would have probably overlooked this prayer had it not been for Wilkinson's book. I will dissect this prayer, as I have done with some of the other Scriptures in other chapters, and I recommend that you incorporate some or all of this prayer into your prayer program. It is small but mighty. I also recommend that you purchase Wilkinson's book to get the full understanding of the prayer, but I will give you a shortened version of the interpretation, as it will be very helpful in your walk with the Lord.

Jabez started with crying out to the Lord. God loves when we cry out to Him, especially when we come to Him *first*. Many times, we go crying to everyone else and save God as a last resort, when He should be first on our speed dial. As I have heard Joyce Meyer say at her conferences, "First, we need to go to the throne and not the phone!" Jabez knew that he had to come humbly, in a vulnerable state (and, believe it or not, vulnerability with the Lord is a great thing)—surrendered and with an open heart and mind to the Lord. Jabez asked the Lord to bless him. Sounds kind of selfish, right? On the surface, I would say so. But you do have to ask God for what you want, even if it is for yourself to be blessed. And who doesn't want to be blessed? There are many ways to be blessed, so here is where I used to get specific with the Lord with my "bless requests." Now, I just want to be in alignment with his will, so I direct all of my bless requests to what God deems will be in tune with what we has for me.

"Enlarge my territory" sounds fancy. Exactly what does that mean? It can mean a few things. Since Jabez lived in Old Testament days, he may have meant that he wanted to own more land so that he could increase his wealth, which would be another category of blessing. You could apply this "enlarging" of your territory to your own livelihood, such as being promoted or owning a house or property. It could mean all of the above. In my walk, I have seen this blessing manifest over the last eleven years since I started saying that prayer. God enlarged my territory primarily by moving me to Pace University, where I was elevated in salary, title, and stature compared to my previous job. Since then, He has not moved me in my position at work vertically but horizontally; I have not been promoted, but I have moved laterally in order to seek new opportunities. As the years progressed, I would add on to this section of the prayer by asking God to grant me favor in those new territories. I didn't want to venture out and not have the favor of God with me!

During my 10+ years at Pace, I have had the privilege of networking professionally, attending and speaking at conferences, and have even been interviewed by the media (television and radio), published in magazines and newspapers, etc. God has opened doors for me to travel and also has allowed me to actually minister in prayer and encouragement, sometimes transforming a career-counseling session into an altar call and a prayer meeting upon the request of the client or colleague, on an as-needed basis. God also opened the door for me to have an impact on people within my home church and sister churches as well. I have attended faith-based conferences and expanded my "territory" by adding more people with whom I can fellowship and share the Word of God. Wilkinson wrote about "expanding the borders." Well, I have crossed a few borders—both literally and figuratively—for pleasure and for work, and have brought the Gospel to people that I never thought would even want to hear it. And now with the publishing of this book, there is no telling where the Lord will take me to minister and teach the Word! So, what Jabez meant by "enlarging the territory" and what we need to pray for can be the same, but I believe we have to amp up the "how" while keeping the "why" in its proper perspective; the purpose is all for God's glory!

"Let your hand be with me, and keep me from harm so that I will be free from pain." We all want the hand of God on us and with us wherever we go so that all can see that we are chosen by Him. It's almost like God is telling Satan and anyone who wants to mess with us, "Can't Touch This," like the MC Hammer song that was popular back in 1990. I always plead the blood of Jesus over my life and the lives of my family members, as well as over the people within my territory, over whom God has assigned me and also over those who are assigned to me. When I say *assigned*, I mean those who God has appointed to minister and sharpen during a season of our lives, as briefly explained in the "Iron Sharpens Iron" chapter. There is nothing like the blood of Jesus to scare evil away, but in Jabez's time, Jesus had not come yet. So he prayed for God's hand to be on him (same concept—we are praying for protection, for God's favor, and for God to use us for His glory). He also said, "Keep me from harm so that I will not be in pain." Since Jabez's name meant "pain" in his native tongue, his prayer would be that he *would not* be in pain and, therefore, would be out of harm's way. And God granted his request. God doesn't deny us as long as what we are asking for is in sync with what He wants for us.

I entitled this chapter "Bless Me, Keep Me, Move Me, Free Me" to help you get the gist of what Jabez was praying. He asked the Lord to *bless* him and have His hand on him, to *keep* him. Jabez also petitioned the Lord to enlarge his territory (expand him or *move* him upward and onward), and *free* him from any pain. I can appreciate these requests and I incorporate them into my daily prayers, but as I was writing this chapter, a slight issue arose for me about this prayer, as I mentioned earlier in the chapter. Although we are supposed to talk to the Lord and submit our requests to Him without hesitation, Jabez's prayer, on the surface, seems a little self-centered to me. It is a very short prayer, and throughout it, you repeatedly read *me* and *my*. The Lord convicted me, not only for calling Jabez's prayer selfish, but for sometimes being "me" and "my" centered in my own prayers (here I go taking the beam out of my own eye again). Granted, I spend lots of time interceding for others, but God had to remind me to keep focused on Him and also to not forget to stay well balanced in my prayer life. The thing that I am calling Jabez out on is the very same thing that God wants me to be mindful of during my prayer time—not being too "me, myself, and I" focused and concentrating on those around me as well. Thanks for the conviction, Lord!

Our prayers don't have to be lengthy; we can't just put in our time with the Lord and think that "quantity is better than quality." Our requests have to be meaningful, heartfelt, humble, and specific. The reason that I included Jabez's prayer in the book is that when you cry out to the Lord, whether it be for your own needs or for the needs of others, God will answer (in His timing, though—remember that!). This prayer, as short as it is, produces results for everyone who comes to the Lord.

CHAPTER 18

Give Him What Is His

Tithing is a biblical principle that dates back to the Old Testament, and it is something that Christians still need to adhere to, although they may believe that tithing was directed under the Mosaic Law before Jesus came. *Tithe* is Hebrew for "a tenth"; a tithe is a tenth, or 10 percent, of your earnings. In modern-day terms, it is 10 percent of your earnings (pretax, or gross, wages) that God is commanding you to give to the "storehouse" or, as we know it today, to the place that feeds you weekly on a spiritual level. For me, that would be my local church, where I worship, fellowship, serve, and get the Word fed to me.

Prior to God's leading me to my home church, I would give a portion of my tithe to two international ministries that "fed me" via television on a weekly basis. Notice that I wrote that I gave "a portion," which is not the whole tithe, so I was being partially obedient to the Word. When I started attending Christ Tabernacle, I still had "crabs in my pocket," so to speak, and I didn't give what I was supposed to give; it was a gradual process for me to finally give the entire tithe. I had a hard time giving up 10 percent (gross) of my hard-earned money to a church that seemed like it didn't need my contribution. The church seemed to have been up and running before I started going, so I wondered, "Why do I need to go without this money and hand it over to them?" There were thousands of people in and out of our building every week, and I didn't make a lot of money to begin with, so I rationalized not handing over the money to the church, which was really not handing over what belongs to God. And, to top it off, I was in a lot of debt, so every chunk of money I had went to paying off my consolidation loans, except for two or three vacations a year, trips to the nail salon, nice clothing, entertainment, and lunches and dinners with friends, which were my priorities. I needed to get out of debt so that I could start saving to buy a house, so any "extra" money was going either to pay my debt or to my house money fund. In essence, there was no room to give God what primarily belonged to Him, even though the whole 100 percent was His because He allowed me to have an income. I also felt embarrassed giving my money to a church, especially that much money, as my family would think I was nuts or that I belonged to some sort of a cult that was taking my money. I had grown up in the Catholic Church, where you were obligated to give only what you could afford; there was no such talk of this 10 percent "cover charge" as a weekly tithe. Why should I go to church and have to give so much money when I had to kill a debt, spend, and save, too?

As you can see, I had a lot of rationalizations as to why I could not, would not, and should not give "my 10 percent" over to the Lord. Well, the Lord spoke to me through a coworker who was a Christian. He told me that the Lord had told him that I needed to start tithing. I did give, but I gave sporadically and only what I *wanted* to give, which was 5 percent of my net income. Even though I wasn't being completely obedient, God started to do something with my finances to get me out of the thirty-five-thousand-dollar debt that I had created over the years. He allowed me the wisdom to consolidate all of my credit cards and also the interest rates on my student loans were significantly reduced so that I could pay only two bills a month with a fixed interest rate. I believe He allowed a dent to be made in my debt payments because I was making a dent in the storehouse tithe. Over the next few years, as I saw Him move in that way in my life, I gradually increased my giving from 5 percent net, to 5 percent gross, to 10 percent net, to the level at which I am currently giving, 10 percent gross. It took a while, but in the process, my debt has been eliminated and I have become a cheerful giver (2 Cor. 9:7 NIV) because I have seen God move in my financial situation, and I don't have that tremendous debt hanging over my head. I also understand God's "economic formula"; the more you give, the more you will be covered and blessed—He will provide if you first give Him what is His.

Tithing is tax deductible if you itemize your deductions. However, that is not the reason that I tithe. I tithe because spiritually and financially, I cannot afford *not* to. I will explain why, but first I'll give you a Scripture that sums up why we must tithe and what God promises to do for us when we obey this biblical principle.

> "Will a mere mortal rob God? Yet you rob me. But you ask, 'How are we robbing you?' In tithes and offerings. You are under a curse—your whole nation—because you are robbing me. Bring the whole tithe into the storehouse, that there may be food in my house. Test me in this," says the Lord Almighty, "and see if I will not throw open the floodgates of heaven and pour out so much blessing that there will not be room enough to store it. I will prevent pests from devouring your crops, and the vines in your fields will not drop their fruit before it is ripe," says the LORD Almighty. "Then all the nations will call you blessed, for yours will be a delightful land," says the LORD Almighty (Mal. 3:8–12 NIV).

When you don't give your tithes, you are robbing God of what is rightfully His. He has blessed you with an income, food, shelter, clothing, education, transportation, savings, benefits, amenities, and all of the extras that are part of the "bonus plan" (vacations and entertainment, which are luxuries and not necessities). God can bless you with the snap of a finger, and He can also take away with the blink of an eye. If we give 10 percent to the place that spiritually feeds us, God will stretch the other 90 percent to go even farther than 100 percent would ever go. And you will find that your expenses will decrease and you will be blessed by others financially to provide for your needs if you obey this biblical principle. In other words, if you take care of God's storehouse, He will provide for the needs of your household. God challenges us in this Scripture to test Him so we can see what a feast He will bring. If you don't give Him what is His, then you will bring a famine on your household. Now, feasts and famines may not happen right away, but again, we cannot afford to disobey with our finances. I don't want to take any chances, so I give what I need to give. Let me share a story with you about a time when I held out on God.

I decided to not pay my tithes for two months and save the money to pay off my credit cards a few months after Christmas. I had completed my tax returns in January and was due a small refund from the State of New

York. In February, I received a notice that I owed a substantial amount of money; actually, the amount was exactly *twice* the amount of the tithes that I was holding onto for two months. Initially, I broke out into a cold sweat because I had never owed that much money to the government. Then, I stopped; I looked at the amount again and then looked up to speak to the Lord. I said, "Okay, Lord. I get it. You want me to pay my tithes, and then you will work out this issue." I understood that this was God's way of tapping me on the shoulder (after picking me up from the floor) and saying, "Give me my 10 percent." I was trying to rob God by paying bills with that money, bills that were not even a necessity but a luxury! When you do that, more bills are going to show up. The notice of the amount owed ended up being the result of a mistake in the way the taxes were calculated on my end, and I ended up getting more of a refund after I surrendered and wrote out my tithing check!

I know that in these tough economic times, there are many people who are unemployed and cannot afford to tithe. Ironically, but biblically, this is the perfect time to tithe—even when you give 10 percent of your unemployment check, watch what the Lord will do for you in terms of stretching your dollars and even lining up the right job opportunity! Some people are skeptical of giving money to a church or ministry because of scandals they have heard about on television, or even in churches in their own backyards, where monies were being stolen or used inappropriately. The Lord commands you to give, and you will be obedient if you do. Those who are stealing will be in disobedience, and God will deal with them accordingly.

As the verse in Malachi says, God can bless your crops and bring a good harvest, or He can allow destruction if you don't give what you need to bring to the storehouse. If you don't sow this financial seed every week, you remove yourself from God's protection that comes from obeying this law. God promises to open the floodgates of heaven and pour out the blessings if we tithe, and I want that blessing in my life. So as much as I would like to save for the down payment on my new home, I have to do what's right by the Father and give Him what is His. He will bring that home in due season if I do the right thing with my finances. So, I urge you to give Him what is His, hand over that 10 percent weekly, and wait for the blessings to flow!

CHAPTER 19

Wisdom Births Understanding

In Chapter 3, I talked about wisdom under the "umbrella" of gifts that manifest under the movement of the Holy Spirit (1 Cor. 12). Wisdom and understanding go together like "The Dynamic Duo", prayer and fasting and "The Twins," grace and mercy. The difference is that wisdom precedes understanding; we will examine that concept shortly.

The Book of Proverbs features the most verses of Scriptures on wisdom and understanding in the Bible. I want to focus on three passages of Scripture in Proverbs that give us practical analogies, emphasizing the value of possessing both. I will not dissect each line but will give my interpretative summary of each, attempting to give you just a glimpse of what the Lord had given Solomon, the author. I recommend that you read a chapter of Proverbs daily because of the tangible, wise counsel that it brings the saints on many core life issues.

> My son, if you accept my words and store up my commands within you, turning your ear to wisdom and applying your heart to understanding—indeed, if you call out for insight and cry aloud for understanding, and if you look for it as for silver and search for it as for hidden treasure, then you will understand the fear of the LORD and find the knowledge of God. For the LORD gives wisdom; from his mouth come knowledge and understanding. (Prov. 2:1–6 NIV)

If you obtain wisdom by "turning your ear" to it, which means actively listening for it from those around you, you will develop an understanding heart and mind. You have to be wise in order to understand what is happening in your life and the lives of those around you. My definition of *wisdom* is "to be insightful, being able to choose what is best in the here and now while considering future consequences and also factoring in what has been done successfully in the past." Seeking wisdom as we would seek treasure, which is high in value, opens the floodgates of heaven for us to possess the fear (reverence) of the Lord, which is the start of our intimate, personal relationship with Him, the "utmost treasure." Wisdom comes from the Lord, not from the world. Granted, people in the world who have not yet received Christ can be wise in their own knowledge, skills, and abilities (KSAs, as we called them when I worked in human resources.) However, true wisdom is a godly gift that only the Holy Spirit can bestow upon us.

> Blessed are those who find wisdom, those who gain understanding, for she is more profitable than silver and yields better returns than gold. She is more precious than rubies; nothing you desire can compare with her. Long life is in her right hand; in her left hand are riches and honor. Her ways are pleasant ways, and all her paths are peace. She is a tree of life to those who take hold of her; those who hold her fast will be blessed. By wisdom the LORD laid the earth's foundations, by understanding he set the heavens in place; by his knowledge the watery depths were divided, and the clouds let drop the dew. My son, do not let wisdom and understanding out of your sight, preserve sound judgment and discretion; they will be life for you, an ornament to grace your neck. Then you will go on your way in safety, and your foot will not stumble. When you lie down, you will not be afraid; when you lie down, your sleep will be sweet. Have no fear of sudden disaster or of the ruin that overtakes the wicked, for the LORD will be at your side and will keep your foot from being snared. (Prov. 3:13–26 NIV)

This passage of Scripture relates to Proverbs 2:1–6 in saying that wisdom is priceless, more valuable than silver, rubies, gold, and other treasures. The world laughs at that because its system places an emphasis on "bling" as a symbol of success and accomplishment. In God's economy, nothing compares to wisdom; no desire in our hearts comes close. Once you have it, all else will follow—long life, honor, riches, peace, blessings, and so on. The Lord possessed wisdom and understanding, and He created the earth, the seas, the heavens, and the trees. Through Solomon, God stresses the importance of never letting go of wisdom, urging us to wear it around our necks like an ornament, so it is with us in our coming in and going out, helping us sleep, walk a safe path, and simply go through life with God's direction.

Wisdom is described throughout Proverbs 3:13–26 and is referred to as *she*. I recall a Bible study that our group from work had a few years ago when we covered Proverbs 3. We had a discussion about why God would call wisdom *she*. Why is wisdom female? Although I can't recall the entire content of the study, Minister Jones, who led it, spoke about women being the ones who carry children and give birth to them. In essence, wisdom carries and then gives birth to understanding. Therefore, it takes time to develop understanding—sometimes more than the nine months that it takes to carry a baby—but wisdom will produce understanding in due season. Wisdom is also a *she* because women are, by nature, nurturers who are relationship oriented, so the more we hold onto "her" (wisdom), the more we can develop that sense of understanding and manifest relationships with others in order to reach a higher level of acceptance of them. A prayer called the Prayer of St. Francis of Assisi includes a line that reads, "Oh, Divine Master, grant that I may not so much seek to be understood, as to understand." To me, this signifies that the person saying this prayer is striving to be able to understand more than to be understood, implying that understanding something or someone needs to override being understood. It takes a very wise and spiritually mature individual to say, "Father, I want to be able to 'get it'—let me just understand and not get caught up in whether people 'get me.'" To me, that is a selfless plea to the Lord, as opposed to wanting everyone to understand us. This is an indication of wisdom inhabiting a person's life.

> Do not rebuke mockers or they will hate you; rebuke the wise and they will love you. Instruct the wise and they will be wiser still; teach the righteous and they will add to their learning. The fear of the LORD is the beginning of wisdom, and knowledge of the Holy One is understanding. (Prov. 9:8–10 NIV)

Those who are wise welcome correction; in fact, they love it! It increases wisdom and also allows for learning lessons. As quoted in Proverbs 3, fear of and knowledge of the Lord is the beginning of wisdom, which births understanding. When we revere the Lord, we are open to correction from godly, wise counsel. Those who are mockers or prideful are closed off to correction; actually, they hate it, and the mockers may end up hating the one who does the rebuking or correcting. Before I became saved, I was not a fan of correction and would even take it as a sign of rejection instead of seeing it as something that would help me learn and grow. Once I came to the Lord and as I developed in my walk with Him, God has given me a fear for Him, as well as the gift of wisdom. Now I am open to receiving correction; although I still don't *like* it, I can appreciate it. God doesn't want us to go around walking out of step with Him, so if someone who is in the faith brings a word of wisdom to us, it is best that we pay heed. And, sometimes, God uses someone who is unsaved or younger than you in their walk to speak a word of wisdom, so pray about discerning this and being able to receive wisdom no matter how God chooses to have it delivered to you.

I pray that after reading the entire chapters of Proverbs 2 and 3—and all of Proverbs when you can—you will ask the Lord to allow you to grow in the area of wisdom. If you already possess it and your "wisdom tank" is running on empty, take the time to refuel. And if you don't have it, pray to the Lord to gain it. You can ask the Lord for wisdom, as James 1:5 (NIV) states: "If any of you lacks wisdom, you should ask God, who gives generously to all without finding fault, and it will be given to you." Remember "the one who gets wisdom loves life; the one who cherishes understanding will soon prosper" (Prov. 19:8 NIV).

Get ready, Wisdom, to give birth to your child, Understanding.

CHAPTER 20

One Flesh, Torn Apart

I was getting ready to "cross the finish line" in writing this book when God put a very strong burden on my heart to feature this chapter based on a text conversation that I was having one day with a friend of almost thirty years, who is in need of healing in her marriage. I can't say that I am thrilled about adding another chapter because I wanted the book to be done already. But I want to be obedient to what the Lord wants me to write. Here I go with another topic!

This is a very delicate chapter and probably the longest one in the book. Rightfully so, because I am touching upon two subjects that have torn many couples apart—infidelity (adultery, as the Bible terms it) and divorce. I want to do these two topics justice in terms of speaking the truth in love, with Scriptural references, of course, because both tear at the flesh of a couple and can tear down a whole household. The divorce rate in this country is increasing each year, which overwhelms me and actually scares me, and I can't even tell you how many couples have reported that infidelity has plagued their marriages over the years. Lord, this is an epidemic that needs serious healing. This country needs deliverance from the selfishness and the lusts of the flesh that are some of the core, underlying issues of both adultery and divorce. I pray that those who are reading this chapter will be led by the Holy Spirit to restore their marriages, granting forgiveness, mercy, and grace in the case of adultery. For those who are divorced, I pray that their flesh will be renewed so that they can move forward as new, complete beings in one flesh again, in the name of Jesus. Amen!

Over the past two decades, I have been approached by people, mostly women, who have experienced infidelity in their marriages. And over the last four years, I have been privileged and honored that a handful of these women have sought my counsel in their times of need. The irony is that I am single, but God has used me to minister to my sisters in need. I believe that God has enabled me to counsel from an objective yet biblical perspective, not taking the woman's side but being able to minister from God's viewpoint in an impartial manner.

I will show you how God works in His own way and how God orders our steps (and how God's economy differs from the natural order of events). For years, I have had people feeling sorry for me, and sometimes I have engaged in my own pity party because I am still single. Relatives and friends constantly ask me, "Why aren't you married yet?" or "What are you waiting for?" Then there was others' consoling, sympathetic reaction to my singlehood: "It will happen for you someday." At times, I would get the "You're just too picky" comment from people because I was holding out for God's best. Even some Christians didn't understand my heart and God's direction for that area of my life, advising me to take action, look into online dating, and go to singles events and on singles cruises, which is not what the Lord has put on my heart to do. What most people don't understand is that I am being cautious, and wise, by waiting on the Lord. In fact, my spiritual mother told me one time that I was wise for being picky. She said that in marriage, you had better be picky because you are committing to a lifetime with a partner, which can be a true blessing or a true curse, depending on whom you marry. She and my spiritual father have been married for almost fifty years and have one of the best relationships that I have seen simply because God is in the middle of it and they work on and pray for their relationship daily.

I am very grateful that God chose me to minister and counsel because I was able to teach myself so much of what I needed to learn and implement in the future as a wife. I was also able to take an honest look at my own selfish behaviors, lack of communication, and occasional lack of respect for the opposite sex as I began to change my mind-set while simultaneously counseling my sisters. By ministering to married women, I was, in turn, gearing up for what lies ahead for me—a healthy, godly marriage. If I would have married in my twenties or even in my early thirties, I would have been divorced by now; I wasn't ready to be a godly wife and a partner in marriage. I was learning from these women's situations and preparing to practice what I was preaching. God used a woman who has been single for quite a long time to speak the Word of God regarding marriage, adultery, and divorce—being a vehicle for God to bring encouragement, restoration, and healing. Only the Lord can do that, and I did His work effectively because He led me through it. I have a better appreciation for and a deeper understanding of marriage and of the word *commitment*. "For what God has joined together, let no man separate," says Mark 10:9 (NIV). Also, I now have a respect for women who hang in there, striving to make their unions work for the glory of God, as well as a concern for people who throw in the towel and end their marriages too quickly. Most important, I have a burden on my heart for people who stray from their marriages because they don't realize the severe impact that their actions can have on the family, sometimes for generations to come (see Num. 14:18, Ex. 20:5, and Ex. 34:7, NIV, for Scriptures on those who are affected, even to the third and fourth generations, as a result of this and other iniquities).

Every situation has been an eye-opener for me. You don't often hear about the lows of marriage from most of the married couples in your family, on your job, and even in the church. Sometimes, people just want to talk about the highs. Generally speaking, on television, in the movies, and in reality, people paint a pretty picture of marriage and may not be honest with others or themselves about the pressures that exist for couples today. Don't misunderstand me—I don't believe that couples should invite everyone into their relationships or wear a banner to advertise that there are issues. Those are private matters. But some people put on a show and try to keep everyone's perception of their lives at the surface level to create an illusion for themselves and others, which is not healthy. And today, you hear a lot about couples planning for their weddings but not really planning for their marriages, which is very alarming, as there is a lifetime that awaits them after the celebrating at the wedding reception. The "until death do us part" aspect of the marriage kicks in after the honeymoon phase is over. Marriage is a beautiful gift designed by God; in Genesis 2:24 (NIV), it says, "For this reason a man will leave his father and mother and be united to his wife, and they will become one flesh." So if you are not married but plan to be, be mindful of whomever you unite with, or "cleave to," as written in the King James Version. And for those who are married, cleaving may have been a challenging process, or you may have done so with a holy ease; either way, the Lord wants to be the third party in that process, so bring Him on board with your program today if you have not already done so.

The women I counseled gave me the real nitty-gritty about being a wife and what the role really entails. Any relationship takes hard work, but I believe that a marital relationship is one of the hardest ones because two people vow to become one flesh, which is a "merger and acquisition" deal to which many couples need lots of time to adjust. Both parties have to commit to be in it for the long haul—a lifetime—with divorce not being an option.

Some of the women had been married for years and had children—one even had grandchildren—while others had been married only a short time and had no children. A wide range of scenarios were behind the infidelity, but it really doesn't matter what the reasons were. The fact that it happened was an indication that something was off in the marriage. Infidelity is one of the most awful situations that anyone can experience because of the adulterer's deceit, betrayal, lying, sneaking around, and generally living a double life. Fortunately, I have never been the victim of infidelity, but on quite a number of occasions, I could have fallen into being "the other woman." God kept me and shielded me from stepping into that dark and dangerous pit from which it is extremely painful to get out. If we are not careful, even the most loyal, most faithful, godliest individual can succumb to the temptation of an extramarital affair. The reason that it is so strong on my heart to include the subject in the book is that we are living in an age when sexual temptations are everywhere, even in the church. We are in End Times, so Satan is working twenty-four hours a day, seven days a week, in order to destroy families, and this is his key weapon—tearing apart the family unit. Satan usually starts with distracting the father, who, biblically, is the spiritual head of the household, although it is not uncommon for the woman of the house to fall into such sin. The spirit of lust seems to be present everywhere we go, dominating everything that we watch on television and see on the Internet, billboards, subways, and buses. The music that is popular now gives the message that sleeping around is acceptable and that there is something wrong with or weird about you if you do not conduct yourself in this manner. I have seen families torn apart by infidelity. I heard a saying one time that says, "The father is the umbrella of the family. When that umbrella is broken or has holes in it, the whole family gets wet." Again, we can substitute *mother* for *father*, but either way, that umbrella needs to be sturdy, shielding the family from the downpours of life. Infidelity does not only affect the two people in the affair but the spouse or spouses being cheated on, as well as any and every child under the umbrella of each family. It really is a "family affair," and the consequences can be long-lasting.

In the Introduction of this book, I mentioned that the word *affair* has a negative connotation for me. It still boggles my mind that we use the term to define this type of experience. *Affair* makes me think of a party or a catered event. Infidelity needs to be called "an extramarital ball of destruction" because that is what it results in for the two people engaged in it, as well as the ones who are being cheated on and the families affected by the damage that it causes. Most of the cases of infidelity that I know of have started as a result of two individuals being very close at work and becoming emotionally attached and verbally disclosing. I have seen many affairs initiate when two people start to connect not only at work but also after work at happy hour, which I frequented myself for a number of years. My personal conviction these days, as brought to me by the Lord, is that even the term *happy hour* is a total contradiction; there is not much that is happy about drowning your sorrows in alcohol, spending your hard-earned money on getting drunk or even just unwinding with a few cocktails, numbing your mind to get away from your troubles for a little while, and then going home to your family in that state, only to wake up with a hangover and the realization that the troubles are still there. One of my former coworkers called alcohol "truth juice," and that is very telling—alcohol lowers our inhibitions and impairs our judgment, and ultimately we end up telling our deep, dark secrets to friends, or even strangers. Sometimes people start becoming affectionate when they are drinking because they have "loosened up," which is very dangerous; it is an invitation to do something when you are in that state that you may regret down the road. I will discuss alcohol and drug addiction in the next chapter, but I wanted to touch on it here as well just to reinforce that, many times, affairs sometimes start innocently over after-work drinks, which is a slippery slope.

As believers in Christ, we do not want to ruin our testimony. I did the bar scene years ago, and I put myself into a tough situation with unbelievers who challenged my faith, and rightfully so, because I was drinking—sloppily, I might add—and ministering at the same time. As it relates to adultery, do not put yourself in a vulnerable position by becoming too friendly with someone who is not available. Be very mindful and guarded when you are in mixed company at work, at school, and at church so that you are not too disclosing or spending too much time with members of the opposite sex unnecessarily, with or without the influence of alcohol, especially if you already have to spend a lot of time with someone of the opposite sex—married or single.

Once, a close friend came to tell me that her husband had been cheating on her for many years with the same woman. The most disturbing part about the whole situation was that her husband's entire extended family knew about the other woman and actually embraced her, which later was devastating for my friend and their children to hear. Even though she and her husband decided to stay together and worked through it, I don't believe that she ever got over the devastation. My initial reaction was, "Well, get a divorce. You obviously can't trust this guy, and how can you ever sleep with him again after what he did?" This was over fifteen years ago, before I came to the Lord, and obviously it was a very dismissive, immature, and selfish response for which, years later, I sincerely apologized. There was very little wisdom in that knee-jerk natural reaction, and now my perspective is totally different. I have to go to God in prayer about issues like these before I open my mouth. I am so grateful that God has changed my heart, and I can now say that my knee-jerk reaction is to advise forgiveness and restoration, which are two of the hardest things that anyone could seek to do after being betrayed. I admire people who stay and work it out; I don't judge them as being weak and needy, like I used to do. Sometimes it takes more grace, I believe, to restore, reconcile, and resurrect a marriage after that devastation than to walk away from it. It is really a bitter pill to swallow, and it is hard to wipe the "egg" of humiliation off your face, but you have to allow God to sew up the brokenness in your heart, manage your emotions daily, and move forward as one flesh with the person who deeply betrayed your trust, taking baby steps. Starting over without your spouse after an affair can be just as devastating and takes a different type of grace to persevere, and neither scenario is going to produce good outcomes unless the Lord is right smack in the middle of the process.

As I am writing this chapter, a song is coming to my mind and I pray that those who need to hear it do so and allow it to minister to the spirit. (Perhaps you can download it on iTunes, YouTube, or Pandora). It is sung by gospel artist Donnie McClurkin, who is also the senior pastor of the Perfecting Your Faith Church in Freeport, Long Island. It is called "We Fall Down," and the chorus is as follows: "We fall down, but we get up. We fall down, but we get up. For a saint is just a sinner who fell down and got up." The distinction between a saint (a believer in Christ who is saved by His grace) and a sinner (one who has not yet come to Christ) is that saints will continue to fall, or sin, but they will get back up by the conviction of the Holy Spirit. Sinners will stay down because they don't know how to get back up yet or they choose to remain fallen. It is a song about God's mercy, about knowing that it is there for us to receive after we stumble. Please note that I am not saying that saints have a license to do whatever they want and simply "get back up," making everything all right and erasing their mistakes. There is judgment and there are consequences to every action for saints and sinners alike. Actually, God's corrective hand can be a little heavier on His children (the saints) because He wants better for us, and we ought to know better due to the prompting of the Holy Spirit within us, but it is good to know that God picks us back up when we fall. It is so difficult for people who have been cheated on to believe that their spouses hurt them in such a horrible way, and it is even more difficult to forgive. It is hard for them to realize that everyone falls, even the strongest saint in the body of Christ. We have to realize that people will fail us but not excuse it or justify it, choosing instead to accept it as a reality that changes the course of a marriage—believe it or not, sometimes for the better. It is devastating to accept this, but once we understand that Jesus is the only one who truly never leaves or forsakes us (Heb. 13:5 NIV), then we can see the people who have hurt us as humans. All humans are fallible, "for all have sinned and fall short of the glory of God" (Rom. 3:23 NIV).

Unfortunately, the betrayed person may see his or her spouse in a different light once infidelity has occurred, a much dimmer light, and it is going to take a lot of healing to make that light bright again. While having dinner with a very close friend who was in this boat not too long ago, the Lord gave me an analogy to help describe how she had been feeling while trying to pick up the pieces of her union after infidelity had set in. I related how she looked at her husband to how we look through a windshield that has not been cleaned in a while—it is filmy, having a layer (or many layers) of dirt on it. How can you see clearly through that glass unless it is thoroughly cleansed? How can you find your way on the road if you are looking at dirt? That is how she felt about her husband after the affair; she felt that their relationship was tainted with dirt—and it was. The mission then was to get the glass, her marriage, clean again, and unfortunately it takes much longer to clean up marital issues than it does to run the windshield wipers. Both parties have to be willing to put in the effort and make a commitment to move forward. However, I am including "We Fall Down" so that those who still can't believe that their spouses betrayed them can program themselves to remember that we fall down, and we get up—and getting back up may be gradual for some. Whenever you want to rant, rave, cuss out, hit, or punch the spouse who betrayed you, remember the words that Jesus spoke to the crowd who wanted to stone the woman caught in adultery (John 8:7 NIV): "Let he who is without sin cast the first stone at her." We all fall down, but with God's grace, we get back up again. So have mercy on the person who betrayed you, and know that God's mercy is brand new every day.

In addition to ministering to those who have been affected by infidelity, I have had friends, both male and female, who have been at a crossroads in their marriages, and infidelity was not the reason for the separation. I am not a fan of divorce (since I became saved), and neither is the Lord. In fact, God hates divorce. As the Lord declares in Malachi 2:16 (AMP), "For the Lord, the God of Israel, says: I hate divorce and marital separation and him who covers his garment [his wife] with violence. Therefore keep a watch upon your spirit [that it may be controlled by My Spirit], that you deal not treacherously and faithlessly [with your marriage mate]." God is not a fan of those who are abusive to their mates and will allow divorce under those circumstances, as well as when there has been infidelity or when a person who does not believe in Christ abandons a believer, as stated in 1 Corinthians 7:15 (NIV): "But if the unbeliever leaves, let it be so. The brother or the sister is not bound in such circumstances; God has called us to live in peace." I will providing Scriptures on adultery and divorce at the end of this chapter to support these principles (some Scriptures date back to the Old Testament and may sound "old school," but we must pay heed if we are believers). Please understand that my purpose for writing this chapter is not to condemn those who are divorced or those who have committed adultery but to show how grieved the Father is when these occur. There are so many Scriptures on these topics, especially adultery; I was surprised to see that when I did my research. God really wants to use me to get this word out to show how much He does not want us to fall into such a pit.

I had a conversation with my spiritual father years ago and he shared something very profound; he said that if two flesh become one and you rip that flesh apart (by severing a tie with divorce), then the flesh is torn in half. In essence, each person in the formal couple is "half a flesh" when they divorce and must be made whole again, only through the work of the Lord. That visualization has remained with me for years, and I use that analogy when I minister to people who are considering divorce. With the statistics being so high in this country, even in the body of Christ, it is important for us to understand that divorce tears couples in half and tears families apart, even in cases where it seems like the most likely or most sensible option. My counsel to those who are seeking divorce, regardless of infidelity or other circumstances, is to meditate on this analogy and seek the Lord so that He, not another relationship or marriage, can make them whole again. Many people think that if they just hook up with someone else, then they will forget their sorrows and move forward. That is not biblical. Wait on the Lord to order your steps, especially after something so very delicate and extremely painful such as this occurs. It may take you months to feel that wholeness again; for some, it will take years. But know that God will complete you, restore you, and renew you, for He adores you!

For those who are married, continue to hold onto the Lord as the third party in your union, as well as keep Scriptures such as Ephesians 5:22–33, 1 Peter 3:1–10, and Colossians 3:18–21 close to you. Please make them come alive in your minds and hearts.

Wives, be subject (be submissive and adapt yourselves) to your own husbands as [a service] to the Lord. For the husband is head of the wife as Christ is the Head of the church, Himself the Savior of [His] body. As the church is subject to Christ, so let wives also be subject in everything to their husbands. Husbands, love your wives, as Christ loved the church and gave Himself up for her, so that He might sanctify her, having cleansed her by the washing of water with the Word, that He might present the church to Himself in glorious splendor, without spot or wrinkle or any such things [that she might be holy and faultless]. Even so husbands should love their wives as [being in a sense] their own bodies. He who loves his own wife loves himself. For no man ever hated his own flesh, but nourishes and carefully protects and cherishes it, as Christ does the church, because we are members (parts) of His body. For this reason a man shall leave his father and his mother and shall be joined to his wife, and the two shall become one flesh. This mystery is very great, but I speak concerning [the relation of] Christ and the church. However, let each man of you [without exception] love his wife as [being in a sense] his very own self; and let the wife see that she respects and reverences her husband [that she notices him, regards him, honors him, prefers him, venerates, and esteems him; and that she defers to him, praises him, and loves and admires him exceedingly]. (Eph. 5:22–33 AMP)

In like manner, you married women, be submissive to your own husbands [subordinate yourselves as being secondary to and dependent on them, and adapt yourselves to them], so that even if any do not obey the Word [of God], they may be won over not by discussion but by the [godly] lives of their wives, when they observe the pure and modest way in which you conduct yourselves, together with your reverence [for your husband; you are to feel for him all that reverence includes: to respect, defer to, revere him—to honor, esteem, appreciate, prize, and, in the human sense, to adore him, that is, to admire, praise, be devoted to, deeply love, and enjoy your husband]. Let not yours be the [merely] external adorning with [elaborate] interweaving and knotting of the hair, the wearing of jewelry, or changes of clothes; but let it be the inward adorning and beauty of the hidden person of the heart, with the incorruptible and unfading charm of a gentle and peaceful spirit, which [is not anxious or wrought up, but] is very precious in the sight of God. For it was thus that the pious women of old who hoped in God were [accustomed] to beautify themselves and were submissive to their husbands [adapting themselves to them as themselves secondary and dependent upon them]. It was thus that Sarah obeyed Abraham [following his guidance and acknowledging his headship over her by] calling him lord (master, leader, authority). And you are now her true daughters if you do right and let nothing terrify you [not giving way to hysterical fears or letting anxieties unnerve you]. In the same way you married men should live considerately with [your wives], with an intelligent recognition [of the marriage relation], honoring the woman as [physically] the weaker, but [realizing that you] are joint heirs of the grace (God's unmerited favor) of life, in order that your prayers may not be hindered and cut off. [Otherwise you cannot pray effectively.] Finally, all [of you] should be of one and the same mind (united in spirit), sympathizing [with one another], loving [each other] as brethren [of one household], compassionate and courteous (tenderhearted and humble). Never return evil for evil or insult for insult (scolding, tongue-lashing, berating), but on the contrary blessing [praying for their welfare, happiness, and protection, and truly pitying and loving them]. For know that to this you have been called, that you may yourselves inherit a blessing [from God—that you may obtain a blessing as heirs, bringing welfare and happiness and protection]. For let him who wants to enjoy life and see good days [good—whether apparent or not] keep his tongue free from evil and his lips from guile (treachery, deceit). (Peter 3:1–10 AMP)

Wives, be subject to your husbands [subordinate and adapt yourselves to them], as is right and fitting and your proper duty in the Lord. Husbands, love your wives [be affectionate and sympathetic with them] and do not be harsh or bitter or resentful toward them. (Col. 3:18–19 AMP)

As promised, below are the Scriptures not previously quoted that address infidelity and divorce. May they speak to your heart today as you read them, and may they convict your spirit if you are involved in an extramarital affair or pondering divorce. Take a moment to allow the Holy Spirit to speak to you and comfort you if you are the one being cheated on, or if you are in the process of divorcing. Let God's love carry you through this difficult time, seek Him daily, and wait on Him to make every wrong right in your life. Remember, He is faithful to do this; only Jesus can make things right. All scriptural passages are taken from the New International Version (NIV); again, some Scriptures sound old-fashioned because they were taken from the law under the Old Testament, before Christ, but I wanted you to see the full effect of what God thinks of both acts. Although our religious affiliations and, for us Christians, our denominations may have different, more accepting than and more modern viewpoints on such, I am simply here to share what God's viewpoints are according to the Scriptures. Know that God has not changed His mind since the beginning of time, so please don't kill the messenger if you do not agree with the following; take it up in conference with the Lord!

Adultery

Exodus 20:14 and Deuteronomy 5:18—"You shall not commit adultery."

Leviticus 20:10—"If a man commits adultery with another man's wife—with the wife of his neighbor—both the adulterer and the adulteress are to be put to death."

Proverbs 5 and 6—Read these entire chapters on adultery.

Jeremiah 29:23—"'For they have done outrageous things in Israel; they have committed adultery with their neighbors' wives, and in my name they have uttered lies—which I did not authorize. I know it and am a witness to it,' declares the LORD."

Ezekiel 16:38—"I will sentence you to the punishment of women who commit adultery and who shed blood; I will bring on you the blood vengeance of my wrath and jealous anger."

Ezekiel 23:43—"Then I said about the one worn out by adultery, 'Now let them use her as a prostitute, for that is all she is.'"

Hosea 4:2—"There is only cursing, lying and murder, stealing and adultery; they break all bounds, and bloodshed follows bloodshed."

Hosea 4:14—"I will not punish your daughters when they turn to prostitution, nor your daughters-in-law when they commit adultery, because the men themselves consort with harlots and sacrifice with shrine prostitutes—a people without understanding will come to ruin!"

Matthew 5:27–28—"You have heard that it was said, 'You shall not commit adultery. But I tell you that anyone who looks at a woman lustfully has already committed adultery with her in his heart."

Matthew 5:32—"But I tell you that anyone who divorces his wife, except for sexual immorality, makes her the victim of adultery, and anyone who marries a divorced woman commits adultery."

Matthew 19:9—"I tell you that anyone who divorces his wife, except for sexual immorality, and marries another woman commits adultery."

Mark 10:11–12—"He answered, 'Anyone who divorces his wife and marries another woman commits adultery against her. And if she divorces her husband and marries another man, she commits adultery.'"

Mark 10:19—"You know the commandments: 'You shall not murder, you shall not commit adultery, you shall not steal, you shall not give false testimony, you shall not defraud, honor your father and mother.'"

John 8:3–4—"The teachers of the law and the Pharisees brought in a woman caught in adultery. They made her stand before the group and said to Jesus, 'Teacher, this woman was caught in the act of adultery.'"

Romans 13:9—"The commandments, 'You shall not commit adultery,' 'You shall not murder,' 'You shall not steal,' 'You shall not covet,' and whatever other command there may be, are summed up in this one command: 'Love your neighbor as yourself.'"

2 Peter 2:14—"With eyes full of adultery, they never stop sinning; they seduce the unstable; they are experts in greed—an accursed brood!"

Divorce

Leviticus 21:7—"They must not marry women defiled by prostitution or divorced from their husbands, because priests are holy to their God."

Leviticus 21:14—"He must not marry a widow, a divorced woman, or a woman defiled by prostitution, but only a virgin from his own people"

Leviticus 22:13—"But if a priest's daughter becomes a widow or is divorced, yet has no children, and she returns to live in her father's household as in her youth, she may eat her father's food. No unauthorized person, however, may eat it."

Numbers 30:9—"Any vow or obligation taken by a widow or divorced woman will be binding on her."

Deuteronomy 22:19—"They shall fine him a hundred shekels of silver and give them to the young woman's father, because this man has given an Israelite virgin a bad name. She shall continue to be his wife; he must not divorce her as long as he lives."

Deuteronomy 22:29—"He shall pay her father fifty shekels of silver. He must marry the young woman, for he has violated her. He can never divorce her as long as he lives."

Deuteronomy 24:1—"When a man takes a wife and marries her, if then she finds no favor in his eyes because he has found some indecency in her, and he writes her a bill of divorce, puts it in her hand, and sends her out of his house, and when she departs out of his house she goes and marries another man, and if the latter husband dislikes her and writes her a bill of divorce and puts it in her hand and sends her out of his house, or if the latter husband dies, who took her as his wife, then her former husband, who sent her away, may not take her again to be his wife after she is defiled. For that is an abomination before the Lord; and you shall not bring guilt upon the land which the Lord your God gives you as an inheritance."

Isaiah 50:1—"This is what the LORD says: 'Where is your mother's certificate of divorce with which I sent her away? Or to which of my creditors did I sell you? Because of your sins you were sold; because of your transgressions your mother was sent away.'"

Jeremiah 3:1—"'If a man divorces his wife and she leaves him and marries another man, should he return to her again? Would not the land be completely defiled? But you have lived as a prostitute with many lovers—would you now return to me?' declares the LORD."

Jeremiah 3:8—"I gave faithless Israel her certificate of divorce and sent her away because of all her adulteries. Yet I saw that her unfaithful sister Judah had no fear; she also went out and committed adultery."

Malachi 2:16—"'The man who hates and divorces his wife,' says the LORD, the God of Israel, 'does violence to the one he should protect,' says the LORD Almighty. So be on your guard, and do not be unfaithful."

Matthew 5:31—"It has been said, 'Anyone who divorces his wife must give her a certificate of divorce. But I tell you that anyone who divorces his wife, except for sexual immorality, makes her the victim of adultery, and anyone who marries a divorced woman commits adultery.'"

Matthew 19:3—"Some Pharisees came to him to test him. They asked, 'Is it lawful for a man to divorce his wife for any and every reason?'"

Matthew 19:7–9—"'Why then,' they asked, 'did Moses command that a man give his wife a certificate of divorce and send her away?' Jesus replied, 'Moses permitted you to divorce your wives because your hearts were hard. But it was not this way from the beginning. I tell you that anyone who divorces his wife, except for sexual immorality, and marries another woman commits adultery.'"

Mark 10:4—"They said, 'Moses permitted a man to write a certificate of divorce and send her away.'"

Mark 10:11—"He answered, 'Anyone who divorces his wife and marries another woman commits adultery against her. And if she divorces her husband and marries another man, she commits adultery.'"

Luke 16:18—"Anyone who divorces his wife and marries another woman commits adultery, and the man who marries a divorced woman commits adultery."

1 Corinthians 7:11–12—"But if she does, she must remain unmarried or else be reconciled to her husband. And a husband must not divorce his wife. To the rest I say this (I, not the Lord): If any brother has a wife who is not a believer and she is willing to live with him, he must not divorce her. And if a woman has a husband who is not a believer and he is willing to live with her, she must not divorce him."

CHAPTER 21

He Came to Die
so We Don't Have to Get High

God put on my heart to add yet another chapter to the book on a topic that hits many nerves and saddens my spirit but grieves the Holy Spirit even more. I was on the fifth round of edits, ready to have this book copyrighted and then published, and I had to put in additions, effectively stopping the press on my editing. This is really a pause for a good cause, though. The topic that was so strongly on my heart, soul, mind, and spirit at 2:47 a.m. on a Saturday is addictions—namely, alcohol and drugs. I have seen addictions destroy families and be the cause of lots of divorces. When I mentioned happy hour in the previous chapter, I thought of including this subject but opted to stay on topic for the sake of finally ending this book. But I would not be true to myself and would not be obedient to the Lord if I didn't pay heed to God's voice telling me that I need to write about this serious issue that is so close to home.

As I stated in the last chapter, I went to many happy hours in my young adult years, and as I wrote in the Introduction, I did my share of partying, which involved drinking. My parents, especially my mother, were always concerned when my sister and I would go out for drinks after work or go to the nightclubs or on boat rides and ski trips. I had many circles of friends, and one group in particular would throw those good ol' "house parties" at our friend's apartment, sometimes packing in thirty to forty people a night (a fire hazard, but a great night of fun). We would also frequent nightclubs. My parents knew that we would be safe because we were either all at my friend's place or with a circle of friends that my parents knew. Regardless, my mother slept with one eye open on so many Saturday nights (and into Sunday mornings) just to hear the key in the door that indicated that we were home. On many nights and mornings, I would find myself vomiting for hours in the bathroom after having too many drinks, and my dear mother would stand outside the bathroom, sarcastically asking me if I wanted a beer instead of showing me a little TLC. I mention this because she didn't go easy on me, and now, years later, I value that tough love attitude very much. She was being sarcastic because she wanted to get her point across, showing me that what I thought was fun was making me sick and yielding bad results. Was it worth the money spent on drinks when I would end up bowing to the porcelain god (aka my new best friend, Mr. Toilet Bowl), potentially damaging my esophagus as well as the enamel on my teeth and the lining of my stomach by vomiting so much, not to mention getting an intense workout on my rib cage from the contractions that vomiting would produce? For that long season, which spanned about fifteen years, my answer was, "Yes!" I kept repeating the same behaviors, time and time again. When I would get better at handling my liquor, I would step it up and drink more, which would bring me right back to my early-Sunday-morning rendezvous with the porcelain god. I would wait a week or two, go out again, and do the same thing all over again. At times—not often, but often enough to put me in the danger zone—my "designated driver" also got drunk and I still allowed him or her to drive me home. You would think that I was a foolish teen or in my early twenties when this happened—think again! I was in my late twenties and into my thirties, which was even worse because I was old enough to know better than to get into a car with someone in that condition. It was a miracle that I made it home alive each time, in one piece, thanks to God's grace. I know people who never made it home because they made a bad decision to ride with someone who was intoxicated, and these people are close to my heart daily even though they are no longer with me on earth.

How masochistic were all of these types of behaviors? I am writing this to show those who are partying "like rock stars" how self-destructive drinking can be. In retrospect, I could have spared myself so much wear and tear on my body, saved myself lots of money by not clubbing and drinking, and not put myself at risk for losing my life in an accident. God allowed me to continue on that path, even a couple of years after I got saved, so I could learn these lessons and share them with others. God kept me through it all; thank you, Jesus, for interceding—and Mama Cruz, too, for praying many early Sunday mornings for my safety.

I want to share with you the root of my parents' concern for me. As I mentioned in a few chapters, I come from a long line of worriers. Well, there were and are drinkers within the family. I don't make light of this, nor do I want to call people out or make this a family-bashing session. My parents were always adamant about not wanting to see their children go down the winding road of alcoholism or drug addiction. When I was in elementary school in 1979, I watched a program with them entitled *Scared Straight,* which was about juvenile delinquency. Teens who were in prison for using and selling drugs were featured, and it really did scare me straight, convincing me that I did not want to go down that path.

My intention here is to enlighten, share what God has to say about addictions (strongholds that we allow to grip our lives), and possibly set some captives free, maybe even some captives in my own extended family and close circle of friends from "back in the day." Too many people around me have suffered health complications and deaths due to these addictions, so this is really a plea to those who still think that this is a not a problem to realize that it surely is and that if we don't strong-arm this generational stronghold, we will be defeated and suffer more losses, passing this tradition down to our children and their children. As I mentioned in the last chapter, generational curses can be carried down to the third and fourth generations if we don't grab a hold of them and rebuke them. Exodus 20:5, Exodus 34:7, and Numbers 14:18 discuss this, so please read them after this chapter if you did not get to do it after Chapter 20.

I must make a note here for those of you who drink wine or beer, not the "hard alcohol," that this applies to you, too. Sometimes people drink those two types of alcohol socially and don't see any problem with that. And some drink beer or wine like it is going out of style and believe that is not an addiction; if this is you, please pay heed to what I am about to say and be mindful of your consumption of these two spirits. Again, I am not writing about this in judgment or in an accusatory manner; like I said, I did my drinking for years, but it never became a serious addiction for me because the Lord, my parents, and I did not allow it to become a stronghold in my life. It did have a foothold for a long time but didn't get to be an addiction for me, praise God.

Wine is an alcoholic beverage that is consumed by many at mealtimes, especially in Euro-American cultures. When consumed in moderation and for the right reasons—to celebrate a special occasion, *not* to drink your cares away—wine in and of itself is acceptable. I grew up in the Catholic Church, where wine was served at Communion to represent the blood of Jesus Christ, so wine is not evil when used in its proper place and role. Jesus turned water into wine at a wedding so that the guests could drink, which was His first miracle (read John 2:1–11), but do so in moderation. One could argue that wine is an "acceptable" alcohol, biblically speaking, but I am not here to advocate; I am here to educate and liberate. Beer is a social drink that is served at concerts, sporting events, and bars and pubs, and it fills the refrigerators of many who just want to have a "cold one" every now and then after work or when the ball game is on. However, Proverbs 20:1 (NIV) says, "Wine is a mocker and beer is a brawler; whoever is led astray by them is not wise." And Ephesians 5:18 (NIV) states, "Do not get drunk on wine, which leads to debauchery. Instead, be filled with the Spirit." What the Word is saying is that if you are "led by" or become intoxicated by these beverages, then *that* is not the will of God. It does not condemn the consumption of them but the consumption to the point of intoxication.

Personally speaking, after what I experienced in my young adult years and have seen around me, I don't think much good comes from drinking alcohol, even on a social level. I have seen many bar fights and showdowns at a family function or a happy hour due to raised tempers and emotions as a result of drinking too much alcohol, even wine or beer. We had a situation at a family party one time when people were actually brawling. Although we laugh about this incident now (it was almost like something out of a sitcom!), there is no humor in people's judgment being impaired, anger being incited, and control being lost—that is what happens, for the most part, when alcohol takes control of a situation. I have a few "war stories" of my own—I even hit someone in the head, twice, when I was drunk even though I had been saved! If we refer back to Galatians 5, which was previously mentioned, in terms of outlining behaviors that are not in alignment with the life that God wants us to live, verse 21b (NIV) says, "I warn you, as I did before, that those who live like this will not inherit the kingdom of God." Drunkenness is a sin according to the Word of God.

For years, God was trying to get my attention in reference to my drinking. He even allowed me to develop a stomach condition that is aggravated by alcohol. I gave up the hard stuff but would still drink wine and suffer some consequences in the process. My sister developed acid reflux and, as a result, was advised not to drink alcohol. I truly believe that God used physical illnesses in both of us to divert our attention from drinking, and, for the most part, it worked. I finally closed the door on drinking completely when the family lost two special people as a result of drinking. The day after I heard of their deaths, God led me to take every bottle of wine in my house and start pouring them down my kitchen sink. However, that is my personal conviction that the Lord gave me, and I do not impose that on anyone. My earnest prayer is that others will be convicted in their spirits to put the glass, or the bottle, down for good. And don't think that I am "wine-bashing"—if you have a dependency on any form of alcohol, you need to get into serious prayer about laying it down and becoming free in the name of Jesus.

I have been around folks who have used drugs and friends whose family members have been addicted. I am not here to claim that it is better to have an alcohol addiction over a drug (substance) addiction, or vice versa; both are dreadful to experience and extremely difficult, but not impossible, to overcome. Unfortunately, I have to admit that I had used drugs recreationally on rare occasions; praise God, I can count the number of times on one hand! Fortunately, I did not really care for the feelings that the drugs produced in me. However, I dated six men in my adolescence and young adult life who either were addicted or had been addicted at one time or another so I have had firsthand experience. It is not a good situation, especially to witness the highs and lows your partner goes through.

Judging from the stories that my friends who have had addicted family members or partners have shared and from my own dating experiences, dealing with a user is dangerous and can make your environment volatile. Besides the lying and the stealing, there is aggression, sometime violence, and mood swings, usually elation followed by depression. In many cases, there is illness—a complication caused by the user's body shutting down as a result of the addiction. In some cases, such situations lead to death from overdosing, heart attack, stroke, and AIDS, for intravenous drug users. What usually starts out as a recreational activity turns out to be a serious habit, an addiction that puts you in a pit and shakes your life and the lives of your family. People think that they can drink and do drugs without their taking a toll on them, but, friend, chemical substances will do you in—physically, emotionally, mentally, financially, and most important, spiritually, for Satan is in control of your life when you start spinning out of control. I have quoted John 10:10 a number of times throughout this book, and it is a key Scripture to always keep on the tip of your tongue and in the forefront of your thoughts: "The thief (Satan) comes to kill, steal, and destroy, but I came to give you life and life more abundantly." Satan uses so many things to steal your joy, destroy your life, and ultimately kill you. In my lifetime, I have seen him use adultery, divorce, alcohol, and drugs as four of his sharpest weapons. Jesus came to give us life more abundantly, and, in my opinion, getting drunk and high are not two methods to use in order to achieve that promised "abundant life." Sure, Hollywood paints a certain picture of the abundant life, but, generally speaking, we see many celebrity couples getting divorced, cheating on their spouses or significant others, checking in and out of rehab due to addictions, and ultimately, for some, fatally overdosing on drugs. Now tell me, is that the "abundant life" that Jesus died to give us? No, that is the life that Jesus came to "set the captives free" from.

I have to share the testimony of a friend with whom I worked many years ago and who has turned his life around for good. He has not yet accepted Christ as the Lord of his life and his personal Savior, but the Lord has definitely kept him from losing his mind, and his life, on many occasions. My prayer is that he reads this and that the Holy Spirit convicts him, just pulling him right into the relationship that he has been missing all of his life. Craig started working at our company as a nineteen year-old with a serious drinking and drug problem. He would come into the office after pulling all-nighters, would get involved in bar brawls, and even got arrested; however, he functioned well on the job so I never had to address his antics outside the workplace. When the behaviors started to spin more out of control, a few coworkers and I had a mini-intervention with him to express our love and concern; he was really starting to abuse drugs and alcohol like never before. God grabbed a hold of Craig's life and allowed him to have the desire to turn his life around. He is in his early thirties now; is pursuing a graduate degree; is drug-, alcohol-, and tobacco-free; lives on his own; has a great girlfriend; and hits the gym and eats right—looks great, too! The point of sharing this story with you is that after he hit rock bottom, there was nowhere else to go but up. God pulled him up and broke some serious chains through Alcoholics Anonymous and Narcotics Anonymous, which are not Bible-based but have a spiritual component to them. I believe that Craig is on the road to living "the abundant life," but there is one very critical piece missing—Jesus. We are going to discuss this in the final chapter of this book, which is coming up shortly.

The Lord wants you to know, through my writing this chapter, that any activity that becomes something that you "must do" in order to have fun or to simply function in your day-to-day life is a stronghold, an addiction, which is bondage that pretty much owns you. If you can't go without it, then it has a serious grip on you and it's time for deliverance. Pray about what it is that God wants to pull you from and then seek godly counsel in order to break those chains. Remember that Jesus came to die so that we don't have to get high!

CHAPTER 22

Watch Your Mouth!

I have touched upon many topics throughout the book, beginning with a definition of who the Father, Son, and Counselor (the Tremendous Trio) are, the importance of leaning on them and them alone for our daily bread, and all of the "side dishes" that come along with that hearty meal—spiritual gifts, special prayers, the combination of prayer and fasting, grace, mercy, wisdom, and understanding. I also covered the different roles that God, along with Jesus and the Holy Spirit, plays in our lives—protector (having our backs), organizer/provider (working everything out for our good), and shepherd (the comforter/restorer who turns our sorrow into joy). In addition, I explained some of the things that we need to do in order to grow in our fellowship with Him—trust, obey, forgive, wait on His timing and will, discern with whom to walk daily and to whom to minister, learn what pleases as well as displeases Him, seek His plan and purpose for our lives, and manage our finances correctly, giving Him what belongs to Him. Furthermore, I presented what the Bible instructs on some very serious life issues that have been in existence since Old Testament times—adultery, divorce, and alcohol and drug use (drunkenness/addictions). Before we come to the close of this book, I felt led to share another no-no in the life of a Christian, but it is so much a part of our culture today that many of those who are saved, including myself, still have a hard time being delivered from a certain way of speaking. "Do not let any unwholesome talk come out of your mouths, but only what is helpful for building others up according to their needs, that it may benefit those who listen" (Eph. 4:29 NIV).

Unwholesome or foul language is something that we hear and, unfortunately, speak every day. Many years ago, we used to hear cuss or swear words only out in the streets, but now we hear it in workplaces, in schools, in our homes, and sometimes just outside of churches. My parents used to say certain words that my siblings and I were not allowed to repeat. If we did, we would catch a beat-down! My parents were not exactly leading by example in this area; it was as if they were living by the "Do as I say, not as I do" model, instructing us not to use "curse words," as they called them, but we were allowed to hear them spoken in the home. In our later years, we all used foul language, especially when my sister started working in an environment where that was the basic vernacular. Growing up, we could not watch certain shows that contained obscene language, but that all went out the door as we grew older, and these programs and movies added to the foulness of our conversations, which is so embedded in our culture today.

Some people refer to foul language as cussing or swearing; as I mentioned earlier; in our home, we called it cursing. As God gave me a revelation to write this chapter, He told me that is *exactly* what we are doing when we speak those words—we are cursing something (or, more likely, someone) and not blessing them. We are also cursing our environments—home, work, school, and so on. As Proverbs 18:21 (NIV) says, "The tongue has the power of life and death, and those who love it will eat its fruit." You speak life or blessing into the atmosphere, or you speak death or cursing. Which would you prefer to have spoken over you, or around you, for that matter?

Two unwholesome words in particular that are part of the mainstream, especially part of urban culture, are the *N* word and the *F* word, and I won't spell these words out. I hear them regularly, and I have to admit that I have used them regularly, too. Within the last couple of years, I have become more mindful about what comes out of my mouth, but every now and then I get in the flesh and drop an F-bomb or two or use the *N* word in the context of a playful greeting, but that still doesn't justify saying it.

I started to really feel convicted of using the *N* word when I went on a two-day retreat with thirty of my colleagues a few years ago. The theme of the retreat was "Internalized Racism," and the two facilitators were very passionate about and equipped to guide us in exploring the stereotypes and prejudices with which we had been raised. One of the sessions was entitled "The *N* Word," and it lasted over four hours. What really started my reflections on why and how we use that word was a conversation that a few of us had with one of the facilitators prior to this main session. We were chatting about how the word doesn't have the same meaning today as it had when it was first used back in the slave times, when Africans were brought to this country by force and were labeled with the word because of its negative connotation. According to DictionaryReference.com, one of the definitions is "perceived as ignorant or inferior," and that's what African slaves were considered because they were not allowed to be educated in this country; many of them were severely oppressed, beaten, raped, tortured, whipped, and even killed by their owners. They were "owned," which is something that I cannot even fathom—how can one man own another man, like property, just because the owner's skin is lighter or his race has the authority? I can go on and on about this topic, but that is not the purpose of this book. I refer you to the Internet for further exploration and research on such a sensitive and controversial topic.

What we were basically saying to the facilitator was that the word is now used as a term of endearment by urban youth, primarily African-American and Latino youth, and is spelled differently—with an -*a* or -*ah* at the end versus the former -*er*. The facilitator's response was that it is only a matter of semantics; the word still carries such a horrific meaning. He also said that the word is in no way endearing, and he gave us a picture of a slave being hanged from a noose, with his body whipped to a bloody pulp and his owners and other people watching and some laughing. "So, tell me," he said, "what is endearing about that?" Well, that stuck with me for a long time. I have to admit that every now and then, after the retreat, I would still say that word, but I didn't use it as frequently, and little by little, it has worked its way out of my vocabulary. If we want to embrace each other, can't we simply call each other "brother" and "sister", or, like my friends use, "bro" or "sis"?

Another word that is thrown around along with the *N* word is the *B* word, which many people use to refer to young women who are their "girls." Literally, that word means "female dog," but again, our culture has transformed the word into something else—it is used as both a term of endearment and to say that a woman is nasty or mean. In reality, what we are saying by addressing someone with either of these words is that they are ignorant or inferior, or nasty, mean, or "dog-like." Those are the literal translations, even though they may not reflect our intention. According to the Word of God, we are not speaking life into those people's lives by using such words but are instead speaking oppression by holding or putting them down. Even after receiving that correction from the Lord, I still have to be very careful about what comes out of my mouth. Even now, as I am writing these words, the Lord is holding me accountable to speak life and not death (which is what oppression is—spiritual death or bondage) over someone's life. Think about what comes out of your mouth—do these words, or any foul language for that matter, build someone up, or do they tear one down?

Now, about the *F* word—this should have its own session at a retreat because it is all over the place. It is part of our mainstream culture now, especially with the reality shows that are on now. They are censored, but every few seconds you hear a "beep" to cover the curse words. That beep has many different meanings, and none of them are good! I have to admit that I have dropped the "WTF" saying that is so popular now (or I have thought it on a number of occasions, feeling it in my heart, too!) Then, there is my "all-time favorite" cuss word that begins with an "s" and ends in "t"; it is not as "heavy duty" as the other words mentioned, but it is still not the best speech for a godly woman to use. These words are such a part of our every day culture that we sometimes don't even perceive them as offensive to those around us.

I was riding the bus home from church one day, and a young Latino male on the bus was talking on his mobile phone. First of all, it is a pet peeve of mine for people to talk on the phone while on public transportation; to me, it is rude and disruptive, especially when the person is not mindful of the volume of his or her voice. In this case, I was appalled by his conversation—every fourth or fifth word out of his mouth contained the *F, B*, or *N* word! I was alone but was so upset for the parents who had young children with them. I have young children in my family and would not want them exposed to such vulgar conversation. Granted, living in our society today, my little "young 'uns" are bound to hear those words sooner or later in school, or even at home if their families speak that way. However, in a public setting, I found it to be so crass and inconsiderate, not to mention excessive. It was almost as if the guy was deliberately being blatantly disrespectful. Or perhaps he didn't realize that he was being offensive because he is so used to speaking that way. Sometimes we don't even have the awareness that we are conducting ourselves in a negative fashion. As I was so grieved in my spirit about it, the Lord spoke to me and said, "Even though you don't curse that incessantly, you had better watch your own mouth!" Whoa! That was a spiritual slap in the face for me. Thanks for yanking that speck out of my eye, Lord!

As Christians, we need to be very mindful of what we speak, not only from a "foul language" perspective but with anything that comes out of our mouths—gossip, back-biting, tale-bearing, dirty or "suggestive" stories, complaints, criticisms, and judgments. The apostle Paul wrote in Colossians 4:6 (NIV), "Let your conversation be always full of grace, seasoned with salt, so that you may know how to answer everyone." Proverbs 13:3 (NIV) supports that, even though it was written way before Paul hit Colossae. It says, "Those who guard their lips preserve their lives, but those who speak rashly will come to ruin." And let's not forget Ephesians 5:4 (NIV)—thank you again, Paul, my favorite apostle—"Nor should there be obscenity, foolish talk or coarse joking, which are out of place, but rather thanksgiving."

I find myself getting constantly convicted, especially in these End Times, when my speech is not wholesome in God's eyes. The tongue is a mighty body part, even though it is small and hidden in our mouths. It helps us talk and eat, two functions that are needed to survive. God's people are held to a higher standard and expected to tame their tongues, especially those who are teachers of the Word. As written in James 3:1–12 (NIV),

> Not many of you should become teachers, my fellow believers; because you know that we who teach will be judged more strictly. We all stumble in many ways. Anyone who is never at fault in what they say is perfect, able to keep their whole body in check. When we put bits into the mouths of horses to make them obey us, we can turn the whole animal. Or take ships as an example. Although they are so large and are driven by strong

winds, they are steered by a very small rudder wherever the pilot wants to go. Likewise, the tongue is a small part of the body, but it makes great boasts. Consider what a great forest is set on fire by a small spark. The tongue also is a fire, a world of evil among the parts of the body. It corrupts the whole body, sets the whole course of one's life on fire, and is itself set on fire by hell. All kinds of animals, birds, reptiles and sea creatures are being tamed and have been tamed by mankind, but no human being can tame the tongue. It is a restless evil, full of deadly poison. With the tongue we praise our Lord and Father, and with it we curse human beings, who have been made in God's likeness. Out of the same mouth come praise and cursing. My brothers and sisters, this should not be. Can both fresh water and salt water flow from the same spring? My brothers and sisters, can a fig tree bear olives, or a grapevine bear figs? Neither can a salt spring produce fresh water.

Although it hurts to be chastised by the Lord, conviction is a great thing—God doesn't want His children getting away with any sin, so He is there to consistently remind us that we are falling short and need to get back up again. He is our loving Father who wants us to edify others, not crucify with our tongues. So pay heed to the Lord when you hear Him command you to "watch your mouth."

CHAPTER 23

His Blood, Your Story

Christ Tabernacle released a CD in 2004, *We Have Overcome*, with the title track featuring the late, great Rev. Calvin Hunt as the soloist. The title is derived from Revelation 12:11 (KJV): "And they overcame him by the blood of the Lamb, and by the word of their testimony; and they loved not their lives unto the death." That is one of my favorite Christian songs, for the primary reason that the choir does a "kick-butt" job at covering it and Calvin sang his heart out every time he ministered, especially with this song. But, on another level, the message of the song is about us winning the race and claiming victory in the name of Jesus. We win at the end of this story, and this book (the Bible) is no fairy tale or work of fiction. It is real! Jesus came to save, cleanse, deliver, sanctify, and allow us to tell our stories by ministering to others who have not yet come to Him.

Although not every saint is called to start an evangelistic ministry, we are all commissioned by Jesus to preach the Gospel to the world (Matt. 28:18–20 NIV). Actually, here are Jesus' exact words from the Scripture so that we know what our roles as followers need to be: "Then Jesus came to them and said, 'All authority in heaven and on earth has been given to me. Therefore go and make disciples of all nations, baptizing them in the name of the Father and of the Son and of the Holy Spirit, and teaching them to obey everything I have commanded you. And surely I am with you always, to the very end of the age.'" By no means am I a missionary in the literal sense of the word, but we are all on a mission field every day at our jobs, schools, homes, and all of our day-to-day activities, even the "soccer mom" who may share her story or testimony with another mom. The blood of Jesus sets us free, and whomever the Son sets free is free indeed (John 8:36 NIV)!

The beautiful thing about the word of your testimony is that it is your story. You don't have to memorize Scriptures or be a Bible scholar to share your heart and speak about how you came to the cross. That is something unique to each saint. As you read in my introduction, my testimony is mine and no one else's. God leads people to Him differently because He knows what each individual needs to experience to bring him or her to a place of surrender. My testimony is not as heavy-duty as some I have heard, in which people have been saved from drug and alcohol addictions and other addictions, domestic violence and other types of abuse, incest, rape, molestation, and God knows what other horrific life experiences. That doesn't mean that those whose testimonies fall under these categories are "more saved" than I am; Calvary is a leveled field where we are all equals. However, I have noticed that the tougher the issues are that a person has been delivered from, the more grateful that person is for salvation and the more likely he or she is to share his or her testimony. This is confirmed in Luke 7:47 (NIV): "Therefore, I tell you, her many sins have been forgiven—as her great love has shown. But whoever has been forgiven little loves little." In other words, those who have been forgiven much will love the Lord much and may be more expressive of that love and gratitude to the Lord through sharing with others.

I used to think that being born again was for the weak, the people who needed a crutch. I was fine in my life, so I thought, believing myself to be a good person. And I thought that born-again Christians were strange. Actually, they are, even from a biblical perspective. I remember my spiritual mother saying to me in my earlier years as a Christian, quoting Exodus 19:5 (KJV), "Now therefore, if ye will obey my voice indeed, and keep my covenant, then ye shall be a *peculiar treasure* unto me above all people: for all the earth is mine." We are peculiar to the world because they can't figure us out! That is because the natural man cannot fathom what a spiritual man believes (1 Cor. 2:14 KJV). Unsaved people just don't get us. They are not supposed to get us; we have to shine on them and be the "light of the world" and the "salt of the earth" (Matt. 5:13–14 NIV). Once that light is shown brightly and they can taste our "flavor," they will want to know more about us and give us the opportunity to tell our story. The Word also says that they will know us by "our fruit" (Matt. 7:16 NIV) so they will want to see not only how the blessings of God are manifesting in our lives but also if we "walk the walk," not just "talk the talk." With Jesus' blood covering us and through sharing our stories of how we came to the cross, we will be seen not only as peculiar treasures but also as victorious overcomers!

Not too long ago, the Lord told me that I have to stand out, even among other Christians. The Lord also addressed the issue of belonging, which kept coming up for me throughout the years. God doesn't want me, or any of His children, for that matter, to get caught up in belonging too much because I belong to Him and can't depend on man for my acceptance. My walk with Jesus has to be so strong that I have to be able to live without attachments. Mind you, the Lord is not instructing me to abandon all relationships or to be detached or void of any connections with man. However, God doesn't want me getting my value from relationships or from being in the in crowd. Also, possessions, titles, degrees, and stature will not give us complete fulfillment; they may give us a sense of belonging with others because of a common bond, but the common bond that we need to concentrate on as believers is the one with whom we report to on a daily basis—Jesus. As I mentioned earlier, I always felt like I didn't belong because I represented more than one culture; I wasn't of just one ethnicity. Well, I do belong—to God, not to man. It is the covenant relationship with God through His Son Jesus Christ that brings that entire sense of belonging to fruition. It took me years to accept that liberating truth. Yes, God is going to take me through certain seasons in my life when I will be considered a "peculiar treasure," even to believers, and that is fine.

In addition, Jesus commanded the following (Matt. 22:37–39 AMP): "And He replied to him, You shall love the Lord your God with all your heart and with all your soul and with all your mind (intellect). This is the great (most important, principal) and first commandment. And a second is like it: You shall love your neighbor as [you do] yourself." Christine Caine wrote a wonderful book entitled *Core Issues* (Willow Creek Association, 2007) that is based on this Scripture. Caine gives a practical approach to this concept of loving God with everything that we have, "from the inside out," and loving ourselves first before we can love others. It is a must-read!

Not only do we obey the Ten Commandments, as brought to the Israelites from the Father via Moses in Exodus 5, but Jesus gave us these other commandments as well—to love the Father, Son, and Holy Spirit with everything we have and to love one another as we love ourselves. In addition, when Jesus was preparing the apostles for His departure, He also gave them a new command as He washed their feet and broke bread with them before His death. Jesus commanded them to love one another as the Lord has loved them (John 13:34 NIV). And, if we love one another *as Jesus loves us,* and also as we love ourselves, "feeding His sheep" will be no problem (John 21:17 NIV), doing so with a holy ease and fulfilling the command of the Great Commission by telling our own story.

So the next time you are approached by someone about your faith, simply tell them what Jesus did for you. Yes, you need to know the Word of God, but people (especially now, in these last days) want to hear honesty, humility, realness—tell them that you overcame evil by the word of your testimony. Tell your story. Nothing compares to the blood of the Lamb that now covers you forever. So, tell your story and, as you do so, you will give God all the glory!

CHAPTER 24

The Invitation:
Do You Really Want Him?

You have journeyed with me throughout the various topics that have helped me grow as a Christian, have read some key Scriptures, have received some words of encouragement, and have read many anecdotal excerpts from my life experiences. My intention was to make the Word more practical for you during your walk with the Lord on earth as you gear up for your "eternal affair" with Father, Son, and Holy Spirit in heaven.

For those of you who are believers, my prayer is that you found this book to be a good resource as you go through life as a believer, perhaps relating to my stories and many of the points that I made. May this book encourage you to come up higher in your walk with Christ, empower you to be all you can be for the one who loves you so much and to help you relate to the world differently, perhaps better, as you look back on where you have come from and where you are heading. Prayerfully, you are grateful to be the godly man or woman God has allowed you to become, willing to share your story with those whom God has placed on your path for you to witness.

For those of you who are not believers of Jesus Christ, your "eternal affair" is about to begin right now. Pardon me for going back into the secular realm again, but I want to make a connection to which many of us can relate. Back in 1998, Latin singer Ricky Martin recorded an anthem for the World Cup entitled "The Cup of Life". Martin sings about winning the trophy and celebrating, and then there is a line that says, "Do you really want it?" I can't say that I really want to win or will ever win the World Cup, but the cup that I am referring to here is larger than any cup from which you will ever drink or any trophy that you will ever win in the natural realm. I quoted this Scripture in an earlier chapter, but I have to repeat it. Jesus said to the woman at the well (John 4:14 NIV), "But whoever drinks the water I give him will never thirst. Indeed, the water I give him will become in him a spring of water welling up to eternal life."

Your walk with Jesus will be the most important walk that you will ever take. It is never ending, it can sometimes be winding, and it is definitely narrow. In Matthew 7:13 (NIV), we learn that our walk is going to be narrow; therefore, people will also consider you narrow-minded. You will be judged, you will be persecuted, you may feel at times like an outcast, and you will have to live according to a higher standard than many of those around you. So now I ask that life-changing question that Ricky sang of over ten years ago, but with a little twist to the question: "Do you really want Him?"

Let me answer that for you, based on experience. Yes! Deep down in your innermost being, you have been longing for that true cup of life that only Jesus can fill. You have tried life on your own, maybe practicing another religion, or multiple religions like I did. I was a dabbler in many practices, and I always came up empty. You tried life knowing *of* Jesus but never really took the time to get to know Him. Maybe you were following Him and closed your heart to Him because of the way life was going, or maybe because of the Christians in your life who were not Christ-like and therefore turned you off of Christ. Now it's time to come back to Him. As Revelation 2:4 (AMP) states, "But I have this [one charge to make] against you: that you have left (abandoned) the love that you had at first [you have deserted Me, your first love]."

I challenge you to commit your life to Jesus Christ and have that personal, intimate, everlasting relationship with the Father through His Son. And, as the ultimate bonus, you get the Holy Spirit deposited in you to be your guide through this journey. You get the three-in-one deal that I have mentioned a number of times throughout the book, and salvation is free! You can't beat that.

Now, take the time now to get into a quiet place, say the prayer below—maybe even a few times until it just brings you to a place of surrender—and open your heart to Jesus. I promise you that your eternal affair will be worth more than anything you will ever have on this earth.

> Father God, I know that I am a sinner. I know that your son Jesus died on the cross and paid for all my sins. He paid my sin debt in full. I know that He rose again on the third day and is alive right now. I call upon the name of the Lord Jesus to save me now. I accept Jesus as my Lord and personal Savior. I ask the Holy Spirit to come into my heart and into my life and help me become the person you want me to be. I ask this in Jesus' name, amen.

Now that you have accepted Jesus into your heart, I want to leave you with two Scriptures (taken from the Amplified Bible) that speak to the love that the Lord has for you. Please always keep these words close to your heart whenever you question His love, don't feel His presence, or the storms of life are blowing.

> For I am persuaded beyond doubt (am sure) that neither death nor life, nor angels nor principalities, nor things impending and threatening nor things to come, nor powers, nor height nor depth, nor anything else in all creation will be able to separate us from the love of God which is in Christ Jesus our Lord. (Rom. 8:38–39)

> May Christ through your faith [actually] dwell (settle down, abide, make His permanent home) in your hearts! May you be rooted deep in love and founded securely on love, that you may have the power and be strong to apprehend and grasp with all the saints [God's devoted people, the experience of that love] what is the breadth and length and height and depth [of it]; [That you may really come] to know [practically, through experience for yourselves] the love of Christ, which far surpasses mere knowledge [without experience]; that you may be filled [through all your being] unto all the fullness of God [may have

the richest measure of the divine Presence, and become a body wholly filled and flooded with God Himself]! (Eph. 3:17–19)

Once you have allowed Jesus in your heart, do not think that you are going to see stars or hear fireworks. Sanctification, or the process through which the Lord makes saints holy, takes a lifetime, so the best way to begin your journey with Jesus is to find a local church, one that is Bible-based, that will feed you the Word of God and where you can learn and eventually serve others with what God has equipped you. Be patient with yourself in this walk and know that God will be very patient with you. He is pleased with your decision, and the fact that you will spend eternity with Him is the best gift you will ever receive on this earth!

Thank you for allowing me to share my heart with you. Be blessed always in your "eternal affair" and enjoy every minute of your journey. I love you, my brother or sister in Christ, but remember that Jesus loves you more.

About the Author

Professionally, Helene Marie Cruz is currently the Assistant Director of Employer Relations at Pace University, New York City Campus, where she builds and maintains relationships with employers who participate in recruiting programs. Previously, she was an Adjunct Professor for the Dyson School of Arts and Sciences at Pace and LaGuardia Community College (CUNY). Helene has presented at conferences and has facilitated workshops locally, regionally and nationally for non-profit organizations, corporations and academic institutions. Prior to her ten years at Pace, Helene worked in the field of human resources for over ten years in a number of companies representing various industries: retail, financial services, advertising, media, and an entertainment union. She graduated with honors with a bachelor's of arts degree in psychology from Pace University and a master's of science in education degree (concentration in counseling) from Fordham University.

Helene currently attends New Life Fellowship Church in Elmhurst, Queens. From a ministerial perspective, she provides career management and self-awareness workshops for the youth and their parents at The Brooklyn Tabernacle (Family Ministries), bridging the gap between generations while bringing a spiritual "flavor" to her presentations. Previously, she has worked with youth and young adults in Youth Explosion at Christ Tabernacle in Glendale, New York. Also, Helene oversaw the Leadership Academy Division of the Organizational Development Department at Christ Tabernacle.

Over the past twenty years, by the grace, wisdom, and direction of the Holy Spirit, Helene has proven herself to be a human resources and career services professional, counselor, relationship builder, coach, negotiator, mediator, professor, facilitator, minister, intercessor/prayer warrior, and now, author and evangelist.